The
Red Colored Bliss

Conceptualization | Compilation | Editing

SAMRIDHI ANEJA

INKQUILLS®

FOR THE READERS, BY THE WRITERS

Published by InkQuills Publishing House
www.inkquills.in

First Edition 2021

ISBN: 978-93-90567-19-5

EDITOR'S NOTE

'The Red Colored Bliss' is an amalgamation of all positive ideologies, beliefs and feelings of people about menstruation. The prime focus behind wanting to compile this book has been to fóster among its readers a sense of 'respect' for the process. It is intended to inspire people to be open and positive about the process.

Wanting to compile 'The Red Colored Bliss' has been a long story. I have come a long way to reach here when I realize that Menstruation is such a divergent concept. We need to STOP associating the process to any negative or positive adjectives. We need to STOP commenting on anyone's Menstrual Journey because each one has their OWN.
Those who have healthy menstruation cycles have their own ways of living with it and those who do not have healthy menstruation cycles due to any misfortune have their own perspectives and beliefs about it.
The main purpose of The Red Colored Bliss is to communicate that Menstruation needs to be accepted and respected like Nature. Now Nature can bring in storms, tornados, cyclones and floods too, but you STILL LOVE HER. Imagine living without the elements of nature, the wind and water and trees and the sun and you'll realize why you should regard the process we are addressing here with a little respect.
That's it, as simple as that.

The book strives to remove these phrases like 'doom's day' or 'bloody mary' or 'blood war' and so many more, which are often used by menstruators to refer to their own periods with that expression of hatred. It is a small trial to question the practice of always representing anyone on their period as 'crying' instead of 'smiling or laughing or playing or simply sleeping in peace' in art, media and literature alike.

With endometriosis, PCOS and infertility being at peak across the globe, this compilation of poems, open letters and short stories is a dedication to all fighters and survivors who are finding their body's way into a healthy red river flow. It is dedicated to those young menstruators who hardly get to see the mighty red abstract painting on the canvas of their undies, who never had any period stories to share among a group discussing their cycles, who often sleep in tears owing to the inferiority complexes caused by abnormal patterns in or absence of cycles and myriad of drastic changes in their bodies. I hope the book makes them realize they're not alone.

The book also boldly addresses the mothers who ask their daughters to be silent about periods, grannies who separate menstruators from God and from their own family, menstruators who shy away from requesting their siblings or lovers to fetch sanitary napkins for them, sellers who pack them in black bags and buyers who accept them in those black bags, people who associate menstruation only to women, anyone and everyone who has stigmatized menstruation.

Some compositions in the book will make you blush, some will give a sense of victory, and some will be shocking revelations. Some might even make you judge your own self and question the jargon you have been using to address the process we are referring to here. I'll be glad if the book hits even just one conscience.

I am utterly grateful to all the contributing authors for helping make the book possible and standing by me to serve the cause of propagating respect for menstruation. I can't thank enough Shishir Kant Bhuyan for making such beautiful illustrations for the book. They are indeed appropriate and inclusive representations of the process.

~Samridhi Aneja
(Compiler and Editor)

CONTRIBUTING WRITERS

The Stigma Enigma ~Prabha Kandhasamy~ 3

Love Had Blossomed A New ~Smriti Sharma~ 4

The Red River ~Akhila Rajesh~ 6

Little Red Friend ~Snover Sanduja~ 9

Bonds of The Red ~Chloe~ 10

Swasth Nari ~Priyanka Chugh~ 15

Missed Periods ~Navneet Singh Bal~ 18

No More Fear ~Sonali Mandal~ 19

Learning The Unsaid ~Shatabdi Manna~ 20

A Page From The Red Diary ~Shatabdi Manna~ 23

The Inner Pocket of His Bag, Safe ~Shatabdi Manna~ 26

If Only I Knew About it Earlier ~Sonal Wadhwa~ 28

She left Him Thoughtful ~Soumya Sarita Kar~ 30

All it Takes is a Positive Perspective ~Vanshika Seth~ 31

Unexplored Life ~Sapna Jadhav Eldandi~ 33

When You Tell Me That… ~Adya Gupta~ 41

Let it Bleed ~Anusha Gupta~ 42

For its Time, High Time Now ~Binnie Sharma~ 43

Because Periods Do Not Bring a 44

Period in our Lives ~Deepti Bajaj Khanna~ 44

Vagina Carriers that Bleed every 28 Days ~Dimple Takhtani~ 45

Red Colored Bliss ~Divya Chatterjee~ 46

You, yes You. ~Gaurav Wadhwa~ 48

And then they will Love You Even More ~Raashi Patel~ 49

It's a Different Me ~Radhvi Kapoor~ 50

Code Red ~Rahul Nayak~ 51

A Gentleman Will… ~Shivam Sinha~ 53

Bloody Human ~Shruti Bose~ 54
Just Ask Your Dad ~Samir Kumar Mandal~ 56
Welcome Back, My Dear Mate ~Sonal Wadhwa~ 58
Beauty of the Red ~Soumya Sarita Kar~ 59
Seeing Red ~Surabhi S Paraki~ 61
Reign of the Red Queen ~Uma Hegde~ 62
The Lesson of Red ~Yadavi Aggarwal~ 64
Love Letter to My Periods ~Priyanka Mohanty~ 69
Yours Affectionately ~Prabha Kandhasamy~ 72
Menstruation, a Gift ~Harshprateek Singh~ 74
Yours Bleedingly ~Ranjitha Ravindran~ 76
Let's Talk It Out ~Sanjana Kapoor~ 78
Communication Matters ~Sonali Mandal~ 81
Gosssh! Men and Periods? ~Tanmay Anand~ 84
Eradicating Menstruation Taboos ~Simran Chauhan~ 86
Dear Nani, Dadi, Mami, Chachi. etc ~Supriya Omi~ 88
Menstruation, What is it ? ~Riya Gupta~ 90
Beauty of Menstruation ~Dr. Smita Todkar~ 92
Period Positivity ~Swati Kansra~ 95

SHORT STORIES

The Stigma Enigma

~Prabha Kandhasamy~

I still vividly remember the day it all happened. It was just few days into my relationship with this crazy and cute human. We were at the hospital to meet a friend and that's when I had this sharp pain in my back which signaled that my longtime friend Aunt flow had come to visit me. The pain started to cumulate and it became so unbearable that I couldn't stand up. I kept my patience and took myself some rest at a nearby bench. That's when he came up. He sat beside me and asked me with so much concern "Hey, what happened?" The moment he asked me, my mind was filled with a million thoughts. Should I tell him or not? If I decide to tell him. How do I tell him? What if he thinks it's gross? And finally, I told him "I am on my period." There wasn't a moment of awkwardness between us at that time. "Is it paining that bad huh? Is there something I can do?" It was the first thing he asked and to be honest I was happy and relieved that I shared that with him. I now stand by my decision that it isn't taboo to tell a guy that you are on your periods and it is something that defines a part of your life. Menstrual health and problems must be normalized and should not be shoved deep into our subconscious mind.

Love Had Blossomed A New

~Smriti Sharma~

Radhika woke up to the sound of the alarm. She turned over and felt something wet on her lower body. She got up from bed and was startled to see blood on the bed sheet. Without a thought she removed it, put up a fresh one, and rushed into the bathroom.

She had her period and yes, she was ashamed of it. Not because she thought it was dirty but since she was a child, she had learnt that women's menstruation should never be talked about with someone of the opposite gender. The day before she was married her mother had warned her that men find it filthy, even your husband might and she shouldn't go near him at 'that time of the month.'

Radhika had been married since two months. Being the only daughter of a middle-class family, her parents were reluctant to get her married to someone living in a different city. They had met Vishal on shaadi.com and after a month of courtship they had tied the knot. She didn't really have a problem with the arranged marriage because she wasn't dating any one at that time and she was almost thirty. "You don't stay young forever." her mother had said.

When they met Vishal, he seemed to be a decent person and so there wasn't much hesitation from either side.

Once she finished cleaning herself and the bed sheet, she came out into the bedroom. She let out a sigh of relief when she realized Vishal had an early morning meeting at the office. Radhika had been extra cautious the previous month to not let the cat out of the bag. "How could I be so careless this time?" She thought to herself.

The relation between both was in the initial stage when they were just getting to know each other. The question of intimacy was far off and period was something she never wanted him to find out at this time.

Radhika was done with her daily chores and having bad cramps, she lay down to rest. Her husband came home after work and she got up to get him tea. As she handed him the cup, she noticed a gift-wrapped box on the table.

"There's something I got for you." he said with a smile.

She took the box to the other room and opened it. She was surprised to see cloth pads, a menstrual cup and a hot water bag.

Vishal entered the room and hugged her from behind. "I'm your husband, Radhika, and there is nothing I want you to hide from me. A period isn't a secret. We need to talk about it often." She blushed, turned around and hugged him back.

Love had blossomed a new.

The Red River

~Akhila Rajesh~

The sky was gloomy and downcast. The evening rouge deepening on the cheek of the sky.
Meena ran quickly to the balcony to pick up the clothes she had hung out to dry. With the same hurriedness she folded them, not neatly, but well enough to stuff them into the cupboards. Meanwhile the grinder's abdomen was churning the idli batter slowly. Meena quickly filled a bowl of water and added to the batter. This too had to be shoved aside before the rain.
And oh yes! The mango thokku - pickle made by grating unripe mangoes. Hastily, Meena mixed the pickle one last time. She took out a pinch and brought it towards her lips. Its deep red colour was vividly reminiscent of blood. Her hand stopped for a second. Then hesitatingly, she let her tongue lick the spoon.
Somewhere a thunder ripped through a cloud and the cloud writhed in pain. The downpour started.

Ram- Meena, where is my blue track pant?
Meena – In your cupboard.
Ram- Where?? I can't find them!
Meena-There only I had kept, just sometime back.
Ram-Ahh, found it! You kept it in the pile of shirts. How careless, wasted my time rummaging for it.
Meena - Oh sorry. Well, I was in a hurry; had to somehow keep all clothes inside before the rain.
Ram – Ah come on, why don't you plan it?

Meena muttered an inaudible and exasperated "How can I?" probably for the 102nd time in her 10-year marriage.
Indeed, amidst all the planning for everybody's household needs, how did she not plan to pull out and keep ready the '3-day-wala' reserved mat from the old cupboard? Now she

would have to wait till Ram did that favour, so she could finally sit down.

Chinnu - Amma, can you please help with this artwork?
Lakshmi- Auyyo Chinnu! Stop! Don't go near your amma. Don't touch her!

Chinnu's legs were faster than her grandmother's words. She was already shoving paper and scissors in Meena's hands – unabashedly touching them.

Lakshmi-Ohh, nobody follows any rules nowadays! Meena- when will you inculcate our customs into your girl?
Chinnu – Amma, you are 3 days untouchable?

Meena cringed and nodded a half-hearted nod.

Chinnu – Sorry grandma. Bye amma.
Lakshmi – Now, where are you walking away like that? You will come right here and touch me. Ask amma to remove your clothes. I will give you new ones. And remember, don't go to your amma after wearing them.
Chinnu- But grandma, why should I change clothes? What will happen if I touch you in these clothes?"
Lakshmi – I will not be pure to do Pooja then.
Chinnu- Then is amma dirty? How? Didn't amma take bath today? If I touch mother and then touch you with clean clothes, how am I passing dirtiness?
Lakshmi- Questions, questions and questions! Today's kids – will not believe in what elders say. But what to say of kids? Even today's women, the educated lot, have no respect for age-old customs. At least respect God.

And rattling off went Lakshmi to continue her Pooja. But her frayed wits made her realise halfway that dinner was only half-cooked. That is, Meena had prepared the curd rice, idlis and sambar, but not the chutney.

Laksmi bellowed from the kitchen – "Nobody should ask me for chutney today! Adjust with sambar.
And for next 3 days, idli for breakfast, rasam-rice for lunch and curd-rice for dinner."
Meena heaved a sigh of relief- luckily, she had had the time to clean the kitchen before the rain.
The night set in for Meena on an old mat near the king-size bed, where Ram was snoring in blissful sleep.

Chinnu – Amma, why don't you sleep up with us?
Meena – After these 3 days, dear.
Chinnu – Why ma, what will happen if you sleep on bed?
Meena – Hmm, as grandma told, lots of questions! But there are as many answers as riddles. Well, nothing would happen, except maybe staining the bed.
Chinnu – Then as grandma says, are you dirty?
Meena – It is not dirtiness. It is just a particular state of the body. But yes, I don't prefer to sleep on bed. But you see, though age-old, there is some merit to some of the customs – like avoiding Pooja and cooking. When the body is in unrest, why bother it with work? This is nature's way of giving 3 day's rest to women. And I ensure to make full use of it for relaxation. See for 3 days now, no cooking, no washing dishes, no folding clothes. No household work for me."
Chinnu – You are confusing me. Do I also have to be 3-days untouchable, when I grow big? I don't want it.
Meena – No dear. Don't think so. Getting menses is just a natural phase of every menstruator. Only our thinking is making it as untouchability. Unfortunately, all this is quite confusing. What is scientific and what is superstitious? Is today's western science believable or the ancient Ayurveda a superstition?
Chinnu, there is nothing to dread…Go to sleep now."
Chinnu – Yes, good night amma.

Meena turned on her side and waded into sleep on her side of the river- a thin stream flowing surreptitiously.

Little Red Friend

~Snover Sanduja~

I wasn't bleeding yet but the pain in my abdomen was a signal of the flow that awaited. The day passed in boredom. As the little red friend finally knocked my door, I grew panicky to see no pad in my closet. It was past 10 in the night. I stuttered while enquiring mom if she had a pack of sanitary napkins.

"No dear, in fact I took the remaining pads from your closet last time"

"I'm bleeding!"

"Wait I'll ask your dad to buy a pack immediately"

Luckily Papa could find a medical store and he entered my room hesitantly and placed the carefully wrapped pack of pads on my bed. I nodded as a gesture of my gratitude. As soon as he left my room Grandpa showered a number of questions on him about his whereabouts. I felt my nerves exploding with irritation with each question he asked. Finally, when they both left the drawing room, I made my way to the bathroom, carefully placing each foot to make least noise. When I came back, relieved that I won't ruin my clothes and the bed sheet, Grandpa called out for me.

"Why didn't you tell me where your dad was?"

Because I needed pads, I thought to myself. I could talk to my grandpa about anything but talking about periods was quivering.

"I'm like your father only. And I wouldn't have worried if you had told me that he was out searching for your stuff"

See, even he couldn't pronounce pads.

"I'm sorry", was all that I could come up with.

"It's okay. If you need anything just let us know."

Bonds of The Red

~Chloe~

Lucy felt light and happy, it had finally happened. Any fear of the stepping stone into growing up was wiped away when her mother explained what was happening to her. ''Think of it as your body is renewing itself." her mother had said to her. Fresh and new felt good to Lucy, she reminded herself that her body is changing.

Her mother knelt next to her tucking pink soft squares into a bag, which she would put in Lucy's backpack, "Remember how to use these?"

"Of course," Lucy beamed, "I unwrap it like a present then put my old one in the paper and put the new one on my underwear!" Her favourite part was getting to wrap it like a present she'd get on her birthday. Her mother gave her a chuckle and scooted her out the door to her waiting school bus.

Taking a seat in the back next to her friend. All Lucy wanted to do was to gush about her new excitement, she did however know it was wrong to brag. Only when she knew Charlotte could experience the joy of this vigorous feeling, would she allow herself to open up to her about it.

Floating the hallways of her junior high school, Lucy lifted her posture in confidence, flaunting each step she took.

"What's got you in such a good mood?" Charlotte next to her asked.

"I guess my confidence has been rejuvenated." And it was true, Lucy glowed in her own aura of personal peace and happiness.

Jumping out of her seat she was reminded of what originated the cause of her newfound lightness. Sneaking a hand into her backpack she took the small, pocket-sized bag into the bathroom. She had a present to unwrap.

Finishing up, she looked in the mirror at her face. Her skin seemed to beam a purity she hadn't seen before. Touching her hair to her braids, she took them out, allowing her blonde strands to frame her porcelain skin. Along with her menstruation cycle, she had an unfamiliar, yet inviting feeling of radiance in her physical and mental state.

Walking out of the bathroom, all the confidence was stripped away when Katy O'Neill snatched her pocket-sized bag of pads from her hand, and to the table, she was sitting with, she shouted,

"Look! Lucy brought her granny diapers to school with her! If you're so afraid of having an accident, maybe you should just go back to potty-training school." Her table and many surrounding it erupted in laughter. Katy threw the bag to the floor, many of the contents spilling out, caused more laughter. Charlotte gave her a comforting touch to the arm, but Lucy burned with too much anger and embarrassment to notice. She grabbed all her stuff and rushed down the hall to the nurse's office.

"Hey sweetie, are you feeling okay?" Her mom asked over the phone, "Is it more than just your headache that's bothering you?" At this question blood rushed to Lucy's face, of course, her mother would figure a headache wasn't enough to cause her to see the school nurse.

"Yea, it's just the headache, it's just making it hard for me to focus in class." Her mom sighed at this,

No more than 20 minutes later, her mother arrived to pick her up. In the car, she sat with her knees to her chest, staring out the window. She knew she shouldn't let it get the best of her, but Katy humiliating her like that was traumatizing. She had wanted to keep her new secret well, a secret. It was something she now had special to her, but Katy ruined it.

Lucy knew she'd eventually have to face her fear the next day at school. When she expected people to laugh and gawk at her, all she received was the same hello's she'd always get. One from the bus driver, another from her friend Sam, who had indeed been at the pad scene, and a regular friendly hello from a pair of twins that sat in front of her and Charlotte.

Lucy's voice was tentative, "Good morning Charlotte." She received only a huff in response. "Is this about yesterday? I know what happened was weird and embarrassing, but I-"

Charlotte cut her off with a sharp turn, "I don't care about that! Why didn't you tell me! How long have you been keeping this a secret from your best friend?"

"Well, I- I didn't want you feeling left out or anything," Lucy started.

"Left out? Lucy, this is something that bonds all menstruators together no matter who they are. I may not have it now, but it's something we'll eventually share and it's so important for me to know we will share that bond."

Lucy was overjoyed that her friend mentioned to her that it was a bond to share. The race or social standing of a human wouldn't determine if they got their menstruation cycle, it was a beautiful relationship all beings could share in!

Weeks passed and no one seemed to care of the incident. Lucy embraced her periods with an open and happy heart. She carried herself stronger than before, and she kept in mind the bond she shared with all the menstruators around her, she found herself treating them all with a kindness.

Lucy offered Katy a hello when she entered the bus, knowing full-well that she would only receive a snarky comment in return. But nothing came, no growl or new mean joke, it almost seemed as though she noticed Lucy's greeting at all! Lucy made note of this strange behavior from Katy.

The day progressed and Lucy gleamed brightly, as she was once again on her menstruation cycle, she found herself more energetic and full of power. She felt her highest and most mature during weeks like this one. Still keeping in mind her own privacy, she made sure to discreetly leave lunch to change her pad midway through the day.

She entered the bathroom hearing a sniffle sob. Nothing obnoxious or big, in fact, the sound was so quiet, it was almost impossible to hear. But Lucy had.

"Hello? Are you okay there? Do you need me to get anyone?" She tapped the stall lightly with her hand.

"Go away!" It was Katy's voice.

"Katy are you okay?" Lucy's voice filled with concern, she pushed the unlocked door ajar and peeked inside.

On the bathroom floor, Katy was sitting with her knees pulled tightly to her chest where she buried her head.

"Oh, Katy what's wrong?"

"You wouldn't understand!" She snapped at her, "You got it all figured out don't you!"

The confusion was clearly evident on Lucy's face because Katy continued with a huff, "I didn't have anyone to tell because my mom left a long time ago!"

She started to put the pieces together, "Katy, why didn't you just say you got your period?"

"Because it's embarrassing! I don't have anyone coaching me through this like you do Lucy!" Something flashed across Katy's eyes. Confusion? Embarrassment?

Lucy considered her next moments carefully, she first wrapped an arm across Katy's shoulder, then pulled out her little bag of pink wrapped pads, handing one to Katy, "I know pink isn't your color but," this earned her a slight grin from Katy, "I know this might sound silly at first but Katy, I'm always here for you, we all are. This is something most females go through, that's what makes it so special, you can depend on any one of us to help you through it."

Leaving it at that, Lucy left the bathroom after explaining the functions of the pad to give Katy her privacy.

Life went on, all of them grew older. Things went back to the new normal, which included secret meetings to ask for pads or tampons, or small talks on the bond they all shared.

Swasth Nari

~Priyanka Chugh~

It was the 10th day of April and Sarita did not come to school. Sarita was a bright and intelligent student of the Government Girls High School of a small village named Tubi. She lived with her grandparents. She was very hardworking, punctual and wanted to be scientist.

Yes, she wanted to be a scientist!!

I being a new science teacher of the school wanted to meet her. I was waiting for her every day. I inquired about her but her friends never told anything. I decided to go and meet her personally. I opened the old register of the school took her address and visited her home.

And yes, I met the genius. I went inside her house; she offered a glass of water with a smile and was a little surprised to see me. I think her grandmother was not so pleased, though. I asked Sarita why she was not coming to school. She kept quiet; I saw her eyes as they were almost filled with tears.

Her grandmother interrupted and told that Sarita will never come to school as now she is a woman. She is not a child now. She is a matured woman and will never come to school as she has got her periods and it is time that she gets married and leaves her parental house. Her grandmother said it was a custom in their village. She has to follow it.

I sat in my office and kept on recalling what I had heard. I went to the principal and narrated it all.

The headmistress of the school asked me to sit and explained that this was common in Tubi as the people in the village were still very orthodox. "Parents think that periods are a taboo, they don't send their daughters, and they believe that the women have no right to go outside the house. They should learn the entire household work and should get married and these girls are not given any knowledge about the use of sanitary napkins, no ways of how to maintain their menstrual hygiene and how to keep themselves clean. They are forced to follow the rules during the days of their menstruation and asked to sleep outside the house. They are not given proper food; thus, many a times young girls die. Every year we organize camps to create awareness but all goes in vain. We try to educate them, Maya, but they don't consider it good. People don't talk about it, even the girls feel shy and consider it not good to talk about the difficulties they face."

Later, the whole night I kept on thinking about Sarita. I thought that she wanted to say something to me. I decided to help her and other girls also. I know it was a challenging task but I was determined to do so.

I had to start from somewhere I decided to take the help of young brigade, my school girls. I knew that it was difficult to change their mind state but I being a teacher never accepted to lose without trying. The very next day of my class started with an interactive session. I started with a topic of "Periods." On hearing this word, the girls looked towards each other, each one with a surprise. I told them how it is a natural biological process and how important it is. I also talked about the hygiene and cleanliness. I talked about all the myths all the superstations associated with it. Girls started interacting with me and asked abundant questions and I was happy to answer them to solve their queries. I tried to pacify them to make them realize that it is a biological process which is very natural and we don't have to cut ourselves from the society due to them.

I kept on putting more efforts after my school hours. I went to the village I met women there and listened to their stories, and the hardships they face. With the help of funding from government, with the help of Aaganwadi members, and also a few female government doctors we started a campaign called "Swasth Nari" through which we distributed eco-friendly sanitary napkins, not only this, classes were organized to educate the girls apart from those at school.

The men and the old ladies of the village opposed us but it was the strong determination of my team which helped me face the struggle.

Our team built portable washrooms. The school teachers and headmistress also donated a part of the salary to make a cemented bathroom. The women of the village started supporting us, women from nearby villages also joined our Swasth Nari campaign and bought us success and yes .... Sarita came back to school and yes, she will be a scientist.

Missed Periods

~Navneet Singh Bal~

I was with a bunch of students at a school discussing about 'periods' with them. They all were 11- to 12-year-old kids and very attentively listening to what I was sharing. After the lecture they started challenging me with all silly, weird, funny questions they could ask. I enjoyed this openness so much because I knew all it would do is to make children understand the process of Menstruation better.

And then suddenly a child asked "So that means my mother would be happy if she misses her period sometimes." I was amazed by the thought behind the child's question as it was not silly or funny. I just loved the innocence and honesty on his face with which he asked me the question.

I turned to him and said "Presently, there are so many sad and difficult problems due to which a female might miss her periods but do you know which a happy occasion to miss a period is? It happens when she holds a baby in her belly. It happens so that she can give life to a new baby like you. Today when you go back home just ask your mother how happy she was when she came to know about your presence and gave birth to you. You'll know what a missed period means to women. After all, we all are just a missed period that gives happiness to our mothers and life to us to see this world full of stars and toys and friends and chocolates...."

No More Fear

~Sonali Mandal~

Fifteen years ago, I got an arranged marriage in a joint family, a totally Indian village set up. Unexpectedly, I got my periods a week before time, this may be due to the mental stress I had undergone or due to the marriage rituals, not sure. I asked my husband where to dry my cloth pad after washing as the ladies' bathroom was too dark and dingy.

As soon as I said this to my husband, he managed to bring two packets of sanitary pads wrapped in a black polythene cover even though the house was still buzzing with 40 family members and few relatives. I breathed out a sigh of relief.

My next concern was disposing the spoilt pad in a village where there was no regular municipality van. They usually made compost from kitchen and agricultural waste. I even discarded the idea of just throwing them in the pond as the specific density of water is more than the absorbent material and the thin layer of plastic, so it may float. So finally, I wrapped them really well and threw them in a deserted place. But the dogs and goats of that village were too curious to see what was inside! So, they brought them inside our courtyard in broad daylight and left them open, finding nothing interesting.

After this incident, no one asked anything directly to me. One of my sisters-in-law showed me a place where they used to burn dry leaves.

After a few months, I was delighted to notice, those rusted tin containers, which were kept on the windowsill with old pieces of clothes used and reused to soak menstrual blood from ages, were reducing in numbers. No more fear of danger from spiders, lizards, centipedes, millipedes and all kinds of insects that had full access as most of tin containers didn't have a lid.

Learning The Unsaid

~Shatabdi Manna~

Her body had seen more than seventy springs, but springs seldom stopped in her heart. One such spring led her to learn English from her granddaughter. The teenaged teacher was strict with home-work and the student was diligent. One of amma's favourite tasks was reading the bi-lingual dictionary that her teacher had got for her as New Year gift. It helped her understanding English words in the language she understood. One day while reading the dictionary, she saw the word 'menstruation'. It was a long word and difficult to pronounce. She started reading it aloud. Her grandson who was playing around, heard her. Excited at hearing a new word that amma was learning, he went downstairs and announced that amma is learning 'mens-too-asion' today. An awkward silence dropped at the dining-table halting a late Sunday-breakfast! The mother jumped to hush him up, the father looked away and turned up the TV volume. The granddaughter leaving food, ran upstairs and saw that amma was writing something in the notebook. Suddenly they heard the grandson crying loudly. Amidst his cry, they could hear, "Nooooo! But I like the word! I will tell this to all my friends! Amma! Amma!"

Amma went downstairs and saw the little boy sobbing on a chair. She took him in arms and kissed his forehead. The grandson told her that he was telling 'mens-too-asion' to everyone and, and… She hugged him with a promise to discuss the word with him after few years. She said that this special word is for grown-up people and should be spoken with much care, love and understanding. Believing amma, he nodded and agreed to the promise that except home, he will not say the word till he grows up to amma's height.

After many years, amma entered the kitchen that day. She asked the maid to hand her the jar of dry fruits. The mother hurried in to help but was stopped. As the milk and rice boiled together, the grandmother got lost in thoughts and memories of her last few menstrual cycles:

'When the gynecologist told me that I was nearing the end of my periods, it was a strange feeling, a mix of several emotions. I silently shed a few precious tears dedicated to the beautiful, significant part of my own self that I would soon part ways with. That day I wanted to dedicate kheer to that phase of my life but somehow could not.'

Her reverie broke with the smell of kheer. It was almost done. As she garnished it, she heard the children fighting over the TV remote. At dinner she noticed, her son avoided her gaze.

Late at night, the granddaughter stealthily sneaked into amma's room. Under the mobile flashlight she saw the alphabets of the word menstruation written several times in the notebook. Mumbling a silent sorry, she kept few pages inside the notebook and left quietly.

Amma sat in the verandah with the dictionary, staring at the diagram of a woman's reproductive system and few words underlined with red pen – estrogen, menarche, uterus, ovary (plural ovaries), fallopian tubes, ovum (plural ova), menses, menstruation, menopause…. She moved her fingers over the diagram, then looked at her abdomen. Suddenly her grandson came and hugged. Sitting next to her, he keenly counted the underlined words, he opined - 'Amma, these are new big words, dictation will be tough. But don't worry, one day you will learn all words of 'mens-too-asion'.

She was about to smile but heard some harsh sounds from downstairs.

'Who tore your textbook like that? Answer me!'

'Where were you? Sleeping? Isn't the topic coming for test?'

'What is menstruation? Tell me? You think it is easy?'

The air was heavy. Amma untied the knotted end of her faded brown sari's pallu, took out some money and called her grandson who looked baffled hearing his sister crying. Kissing his cheek, she tenderly asked him to bring Fahbicol (Fevicol, a popular adhesive brand in India) and chaaklet (chocolates) for the siblings. As he came downstairs, the air from verandah carried the words – f-e-m-a-l-e – b-o-d-y, e-s-t-r-o-g-e-n, o-v-u-m, m-e-n-s-t-r-u-a-t-i-o-n…

A Page From The Red Diary

~Shatabdi Manna~

As the train started moving, they smilingly waved at each other.

After returning to the flat, he locked the door from inside, headed towards the bedroom and stared at the side-table drawer. This had always been locked. However, this time it wasn't. He hesitantly took out a thick, red diary from the drawer and sat on the bed. He loved her and the poems. She mostly shared them with him but he somehow believed that 'more' poems were in the diary. Was he breaking his promise now? After much doubt and guilt, he consoled himself reminding her words - "You would never ask me to show my diary to you." He had not asked her. He had got the diary himself.

Long-awaited curiosity and excitement made him forget everything that day as he got engrossed in reading. The entire week, he continued flipping pages. There were poems indeed - about her ponderings on various things, about friends, family-members, some were about him, some described the initial days of their meeting; he knew these, but read them again. A small unfinished poem was about the first kiss, written on one of his birthdays. He felt overwhelmed. She would never tell him about it in words. He only knew about it through her eyes. The diary had many other things too. Long notes related to study, work, unsent letters written to various family-members and so on. There were proses as well. He smiled. He didn't know about this. And there were typical entries, starting with the words – Dear diary. Suddenly an old entry broke his flow of thoughts.

"I hate myself. I hate the blood. I hate everyone. What have I done to be punished like this? I cried so much for just having a piece of my favourite mango-pickle but they scolded me. I was slapped for almost entering the pooja-ghar, this was done so that I remember it forever and never attempt this again. I cannot sit, eat or sleep. Blood is coming from my down and my stomach pains. I do not know why! There was blood on my frock in the morning, now there is a spot on the bed-sheet. Bhai came to ask what happened to me but was dragged away and was told loudly that he should not meet me for a week now. I could hear him crying and asking why so? I cried too. Nobody listened.

My food is changed. The new food is bland. Mutton has been cooked in the house today but I haven't got any of it. Long torn pieces of old saris have been given to me to use for soaking up the blood flowing from down.

Just now maa had come. At times she was angry on my questions, at times she cried. I don't understand what's happening. I can hear the discussions about whether I should now be sent to the school or not. Sarita doesn't come to school anymore. Is she also crying?"

He read all, till the end. The diary started from the last page. It was a thick bundle of loose sheets that continued till now. She keeps adding pages.

He remembered many years ago his younger sister was isolated almost in the same way. Initially he tried meeting her but was stopped. Since then, eventually his sister had started distancing herself from the family for few days every month and gradually, this became normal. He remembered she did not join the pooja conducted in the village-temple for his successful graduation. Had someone slapped her too?

He cried silently. He went to the bathroom and opened the cupboard. Only two sanitary napkins.

Next day after cooking, he called his sister. After customary talks, gathering much courage, he said all that he wanted to. He apologized for being busy with his studies and football most of the time, as she dealt with her periods and the pain almost alone. Tears rolled down the sister's cheeks. Before keeping down the phone-receiver she said that she would never stop her son from meeting his sister.

In the evening, he headed towards the New Delhi station. She was returning. Both were happy. On their way back, they picked essential things from the neighbourhood grocery-store.

While sorting the grocery-items, she saw a brown packet and was surprised to see sanitary napkins inside it of almost all sizes. Taking one of them, she went to him. He was opening the mango-pickle jar. Leaving the jar half-opened, he held her hand and took her to the bedroom. The diary was on the side-table. Nervous and silent, he sat down on the bed. She slowly came near and held his face.

As they served each other dinner, she told him about one thing that wasn't in the diary.

Once she had an important presentation at the city-college. She requested her mother to get sanitary napkins just once as she was traveling outside. Mother sternly refused saying it was not possible to get sanitary napkins exclusively for her in a house that had eight women! All of them used cloth. She had felt asleep sobbing that night. Two days later, inside the side-table drawer near her bed, she saw a black polythene, inside which there was something wrapped in newspaper. Tearing those wrappings, she was surprised to see a packet of sanitary napkins! She had felt like shouting from the roof clasping the packet close to her heart!

He was very surprised and asked who had got that amidst such risk. She smiled saying, 'Maa never told'.

He asked again – 'Still, any guesses'? Biting a piece of pickle, she said – 'Maybe yes, maybe no, maybe the shadow behind curtain that day'!

The Inner Pocket of His Bag, Safe

~Shatabdi Manna~

With great precision she was drawing the labelled diagram of a woman's reproductive system on the black-board with a piece of chalk. A murmur erupted, giggles were heard, some embarrassed faces looked away from the diagram in progress. Unperturbed, the elderly teacher continued drawing, along with explaining terms associated with the human reproductive system. The whispers grew louder when she was explaining menstruation. It irked her and she slammed the wooden duster on desk. Voices faded and pin drop silence played around. She asked in a firm voice – 'Can anyone of you tell me what I was explaining just now?' Silence was the reply. She repeated the question. A boy from the middle row answered in feeble voice – 'Menstruation'. Giggles emerged again. The teacher slammed the duster once more. Addressing the boy, she asked – 'Yes. Right. Can you tell the class what is menstruation'? Raghav, though nervous, answered the question correctly. 'Very good, sit down' - said the teacher. Continuing the class for some time, she left when the bell for lunch announced a break.

Raghav was going to wash his hands when someone chuckled looking at him. More students joined the laugh. As he sat down to eat, one of them mocking the teacher's voice asked – 'Can you tell the class what is menstruation'? The collective laughter pierced him like needles. Someone said – 'Today's topic is his favourite'! Another student asked – 'So what is your favourite part of a woman's down system, huh'? He felt as if his stomach writhed in pain. He somehow gulped down the morsels with water. He could not concentrate on rest of the classes after this.

At home, looking at the diagram in the textbook, he kept wondering. What was so wrong in defining menstruation? What if it had come as a question in exam? Students would have written answer to that. So why were they laughing? What is so wrong if I was listening carefully in today's class? I do so in all classes.

Next day as he went to his desk, he saw a small packet. He was surprised. As he removed the baby pink wrapper; he saw a folded sanitary napkin. There was a small chit on it with the words – You know better about it! The bunch of students around him started laughing.

At evening when Arjun, his elder brother came to call him for a cricket match in the colony, he refused to go. Despite coaxing several times, he didn't budge from the bed. Arjun sat down and turned around his face. He was right, his brother was crying.

As Raghav narrated the incidents of school, he said – 'How and why am I being laughed at if I spoke about menstruation?'

'She was in our class. Soft-spoken like you. We were in VIII. One day few blood spots were visible on her white uniform. She was not aware of that, perhaps. One of her friends quickly got up from her seat and rushed to her with something wrapped in paper. The girl almost turned pale as she turned around to look at her uniform. She immediately rushed towards the washroom. Few other girls ran towards her with pieces of chalk to help her cover the blood stains. After that she never came to the school.' added Arjun.

Raghav sat straight and asked – 'But why did she leave the school'?

'Menstruation and spots are big deal here, it's a tragic reality.' and there was silence.

Raghav slowly got up from the bed and kept back the textbook in his bag. The sanitary napkin in the pink cover along with the chit was lying in the inner pocket of his bag, safe, the only difference being he did not hate it anymore. He thought he could give it to any of his classmates who was in need of it.

If Only I Knew About it Earlier

~Sonal Wadhwa~

I did not even have the slightest idea that the day would change the entire course of my life. In the next few hours, I was about to enter adulthood. It was a hard day for me considering the way I learnt about periods.

I was writing my exam when I started to feel some liquid flowing outside from my body. Yes, like many other Indian mothers, my mother had given me no intimation that something like this was bound to happen at my age. I knew nothing about menstruation. I went to the washroom with a hope that everything was alright. But as I entered, what I saw on my underwear was blood. I had seen blood many times earlier because I was used to falling while playing. But the place this blood was coming from today was enough to get me into a panic state. I washed my private area and went back to class. Blood started dripping again. When I got up to leave after exam, I saw that my seat had blood on it. I did not have anything to wipe it with so I used my school skirt and started walking towards the bicycle stand to go back home. What I did not think about was the 300m walking distance to my bicycle with hundreds of students walking behind me, hence those stares.

Thankfully, one of my friends was passing by. I told her that girls were staring at me. She then got to notice my skirt and the next second was right behind me asking me to keep walking that way until we reached my cycle.

I knew she would be at the shop helping my father, so I went there first. I did not get down from my cycle and told her what happened at school. At least then she could have told me about periods. But no, she handed me a pack of sanitary napkins and said, "Go home, take a bath and use this. I will come home after some time and we will talk more." I managed to use the given resources with whatever little my mind could explain. Not knowing what better to do, I went to my neighbour's place. I was playing there when a boy spotted blood on my jeans and told me I was dirty, and I am not allowed to play with them. Even the other kids started laughing at me. We were all between 12 and 15, so I cannot blame them today for what happened. Feeling too embarrassed for people laughing at me twice in a single day, I left and cried as I went back home, feeling really dirty and blaming God why he was doing that to me.

My mother returned in a few hours and saw me in a miserable state, all messed up and crying. I narrated the entire story from school to the neighbouring kids. She consoled and explained everything she could regarding the process.

This was a discovery I was not yet ready to accept. I was angry at what had happened.

14 years from then, of course I do not feel the same way about periods today. They are as much a part of my life as food and water and there is nothing to be sad or angry about it. On the contrary, now when my dates waver, I feel afraid. I feel happy when I get them every month because they symbolize a healthy body. I would encourage all mothers to talk to their children freely about menstruation.

She left Him Thoughtful

~Soumya Sarita Kar~

Doorbell rang. Rupesh, with much wonder about who could be there at this time of the day, opened the door. Ruchika, standing there with face flushed and smeared with tear was sobbing uncontrollably. She entered past him and Rupesh's eyes were widened at the sight of a deep red stain on her white skirt.

Though he understood the situation, he could not talk about it to her. Asking her to stay there he rushed to the house next door to fetch their neighbor, Neelam aunty to help Ruchika as their granny had been out of town for a few days.

Ruchika followed whatever Neelam aunty asked her to do. Meanwhile Neelam aunty addressed Rupesh with a lot of disappointment, "Menstruation is nothing shameful to discuss, and you, being an adult as well as a Science student should not have hesitated to comfort Ruchika when she was panicking and crying. This whole process of menstruation is not related to only women; it's the very source of life; menstruation, basically, is all about fertility and reproduction. Then what's so shameful and weird or awkward discussing it!

It is unbelievable how belonging to the region where menstruation is celebrated with festivities, you are shy of addressing it."

"Now make sure you take care of her." she left Rupesh thoughtful after handing a pack of sanitary napkins to him.

All it Takes is a Positive Perspective

~Vanshika Seth~

'PERIODS- Shhh don't speak that word so loudly',

'I am on my period today - Then you better don't roam around the class and keep sitting'

'Hey please check if there's any stain on my skirt – No, no there's no stain, don't worry'

'Do you have a pad? - Yes, come close put it in your pocket carefully.'

That's how high school girls were supposed to be when it came to periods. They were taught to be all secretive and quiet about it. And how can someone forget the sessions where you were taken to a classroom completely free of boys and were lectured about menstruation.

So, like any other high school girl, there was this girl who was completely shy talking about periods. She never used to speak it out loud and whenever the topic of menstruation was explained in the class, she kept her eyes to herself and avoided changing gestures with anybody.

In class 7, one of her best friends had a red stain on her skirt and she thought it was red paint because their art class just got over. So, she casually told her friend, "Hey you got some red paint spilled on your skirt." On hearing that her friend got conscious and immediately ran to the washroom. She didn't understand what was so wrong.

That day she saw a 'PAD' for the first time in her life when her friend told her that it was not a casual red stain but her period bloodstain. Confused, she immediately ran to her mother upon reaching home and told her about what happened at the school. Her mother figured it was the right time to enlighten her daughter about periods and so she told her everything about them.

Since then, all her friends started to get their periods one by one but she didn't. What she got was a growing problem called 'Acne'. Her face got ruined and everybody used to make fun of her. On consulting a doctor, it came out that due to not getting periods there was some hormonal imbalance which had led to acne. She got flushed and frustrated. She refused to look at herself in the mirror, began avoiding all the parties and get-togethers, and used to cry all day long.

This led her to blame periods for her condition. She developed a sense of negativity towards the process for putting her in such a crisis and ruining her face. She had reached class 9 and still didn’t get her first period. But across half of grade 9 she got her first period. She was not happy at all and still continued to hate periods.

But gradually, things began to change in her favor, her skin started to become clearer and it glowed, she started to regain her lost confidence. The negativity for menstruation which she had held in her mind started to shift to positivity when she learnt about the beauty of it.

Presently that girl is working with an NGO running a campaign for menstrual hygiene and positivism; visiting schools, and educating both boys and girls about the beauty of menstruation. And that insecure, meek and unassertive girl, now with more confident, bold, and positive traits is me.

Developing a positive approach towards periods made me realize that it is a blessing not a curse, that it is normal not odd, that it is beautiful not awful.

Unexplored Life

~Sapna Jadhav Eldandi~

The arrival of this long-awaited envelope filled my heart with profound bliss. As I read my name on its cover, I unsealed the envelope in the next few seconds. My heart was beating faster than usual. I calmed myself, took a deep breath and witnessed something that I often dreamt of.

It was an appointment letter for the post of an assistant photographer from the "Wild Habitat Channel" – the same channel that inspired me to take up wildlife photography as my passion and profession equally. It deeply rooted the stems of capturing the diverse moments of animals in my heart, with the guidance of the lens that display sheer magic. I used to watch these animals for hours as a kid when other children of my age were busy watching cartoons. This fascinating life of animals away from periphery of the humans was my destination.

I was given my first assignment to the Sumatra Island which is located in western Indonesia. I was asked to report to the office in the next seven days which flew away with the blink of an eye. My excitement had no boundaries. I was sure that my life was about to transform with this new venture in my hands.

After flying for some thousands of kilometers from India, I reached the much-anticipated venue.

"Ms. Amreen Siddiqui, welcome onboard" ... I was received with a warm hug by Ms. Hazel George. She was the Assistant Editor of the Channel. Her gesture transmitted extremely good vibes in this unfamiliar country. We knew each other as we had exchanged a couple of phone calls in last few days after my recruitment in the channel. To my surprise she was my room partner too, that added as an icing on my cake.

After a week of efficient homework by the team for our upcoming assignment for the Sumatra islands, we were all set to go on the field. I was stunned with the background preparations that takes to make any project productive and successful. I was too amateur to this world of reality. My exposure to wildlife and their way of living was almost zero. There was so much to seek and explore in this vast space of wild life. I was looking forward to some life evolving experiences which were on my way.

The theme for this project was "Unexplored Life". I was super nervous but at the same time on my toes to impart my best. And why not, as I was waiting for this opportunity all my life. I can't afford to perform like a mediocre this time. I have to give away everything that I have. With all this motivation and positivity, I walked down the aisle leading to the land of greenery that would eventually lead me towards the fruitful bliss.

It was our first day at Sumatra Island and the crew was super excited for this upcoming thrill. We started our journey towards the thick forest before the arrival of the sun. I wanted to witness and capture something that was never seen before. My morale was very high, and I was confident about my capabilities. As we walked for around 3.5 kilometers through the dense trees and unknown silence, something knocked my mind. I turned around but couldn't spot anything. I ignored the calling of my heart and proceeded towards the never-ending path.

As we took a small halt, I heard a slight chirping. I adjusted the lens of my camera and without anyone's knowledge continued to follow in the direction of that sound. As I took around fifty steps ahead, I witnessed a soulful sight. It was a Sumatran Ground Cuckoo. It's one of the rare species to be found around the world. They are sparsely sighted because of their limited number. I controlled my excitement and concentrated on the lens. So that I don't divert her attention and can get few marvelous shots. I captured some of the vivid moments of the bird as if a super model was posing for some exclusive photo shoot. The shots that I would remember for the long time. It was unique and real. It gives extreme peace and sense of satisfaction to a photographer when he clicks the soul of the moment which will pass by and never come back. The birds are always true and genuine when they are in their habitat. Capturing them in their authentic environment was an ultimate bliss.

"Hey Amreen, what are you doing here? We have been looking for you since long" … Hazel interrupted my chain of thoughts.

The bird flew away the next second as Hazel proved her presence in a steady tone.

"Look what I have clicked" … I tilted my camera so that she can see the pictures properly.

"Oh wow, that's a Ground Cuckoo. I was seeking her since ages but never got to spot her. Lucky You" … Hazel commented.

"I am so joyous for you, May God Bless you with may such offerings" ... She added.

"Thank you so much Hazel, it means a lot for a novice like me. Let's go back and have a cup of black coffee" … I insisted

"Of course, accompanied by your Gujiya's (Indian sweet) from Made in India." … She said winking her left eye.

As I rested myself on the bed that night, the mesmerizing scenes of the morning flashed in front of my eyes. The innocent movements of the cuckoo, its fragile yet strong feathers and full of life attitude took me back to the forest once again. The bird's soothing and rejuvenating voice had the capability to heal a wounded heart. Today's experience filled my heart with confidence and positivity. I assured myself to work hard to accomplish my ultimate goal. With these varied thoughts, I dozed off.

It was around a week; days flew away swiftly that I didn't even realize. I clicked so many special moments of the birds and animals. I was happy with my work but still not satisfied. I was waiting for that extra-ordinary shot that was yet to be captured.

Next morning, I thought of taking a walk around the vicinity, but somehow, I crossed the boundary line of our accommodation which I was not supposed to do. My feet anonymously chose the path towards the habitat that doesn't come in our limitations. But I didn't stop myself from moving ahead towards the undesired destination. Although I was warned by the local people not to cross that way as there were resent paranormal activities witnessed by the people, but still I did. As I walked and walked deep inside, I felt the connection with the ambience. There was purifying peace felt in the lap of this God blessed nature.

"There can't be anything wrong here" … I assured myself

As I got indulged clicking the random pictures, I encountered something that I never thought of. There she was! I was shocked by what I just saw. "Maybe she needs help, let me rescue her" … I said to myself. I tried to approach her but some weird force in me stopped me from doing the same. My thoughts and feet didn't sync with each other and I was stunt for next few seconds with what was happening in front of me. She was mourning as if something was pricking her deep till the core. Her agony was evident from her body language. I couldn't resist myself anymore and took a step to help her ignoring everything else that was distracting my mind. The moment I went near her, she looked straight into my eyes with the hope of healing. Her gaze was firm and steady like a rock. She was looking for a ray of hope that will rescue her pain. She was helplessly lying on the thick bed of dry leaves and scattered twigs.

As, I leaned forward to examine what has happened to her, I was shocked. There was a discharge of blood from her body. "She must have encountered a wild animal" ... I thought.

I tried to discover her wound, but somehow, I couldn't find it. On the other hand, she was very well responding to my touch. After few minutes of exploring, I carefully touched and noticed something that I never thought of. She was bleeding through her vagina. I was stunned when I realized that she was going through her menstruation cycle. I held her close to me and tried soothing her with my gentle touch. The sense of comfort made her feel better. I have heard many stories about the sensitivity and belongingness of animals, but today I was experiencing it. It was difficult for me to accept the fact that I was actually soothing a Gibbon.

Yes… you heard it right. She was not a girl or a lady, rather she was an Ape. Gibbons comes from the ape family. She was as gorgeous as any super model. A furry white gibbon was exactly in front of my eyes, she was soft and vulnerable. Again, a rare of its kind. Although I have read about these primates in my research, before I resumed this project. I also knew the fact that only few species of animals other than primates have menstrual cycle and they actually bleed during this period. But I never thought in my life that I will get to perceive something like this in real. This was surreal.

"Hey Amreen" …. Hazel arrived.

"Shhh." … I stopped her placing a finger on my lips.

She understood my gesture and stood away maintaining a distance assuring not to disturb the animal. She kept watching her movements. Hazel was awestruck as it was not a familiar sight to be witnessed.

It was around three hours that I was with her and now she showed a sign of slight movement to get up and go back to her family. She made an effort and stood up. I guess…she must have been left alone due to her sudden discharge that didn't allow her to catch up with the speed of her fellow mates. I assisted her and she was all set to bid a goodbye to me. I kept watching her as she climbed the pine tree in no time. Within next few minutes she leaped from one tree to another and disappeared into the wild.

Hazel and I hugged each other and the silence between us spoke a thousand words.

The red bliss that most females go through for most of their lives must be respected and celebrated.

We often talk about the pain and sufferings of mankind but never give emphasis to this side of wild life. I came to this island with the motive of excelling in my profession but to my surprise, I didn't click any pictures of this infrequent ape. But yes, her portrait rested in my memory forever.

There are unique creations of the Almighty spread all over the universe. They all have equal share and rights on this earth as we human beings do. We mankind, must respect this creativity of the God. He is the father of all those who exist on our planet and loves everyone equally. This unfamiliar gibbon crossed my path to mark her existence.

I don't know whether this official trip to Sumatra island was successful or not, I don't know whether I achieved that perfect picture of my life, but I was quite sure that I had explored the "Unexplored Life."

POETRY

When You Tell Me That...

~Adya Gupta~

When you tell me that the blood between my legs stands between me and my God, I want to shout to your face that the creator of my body would never wish for me to stay away from Him because of my body.

I want to talk sense into you when you tell me to hide my sanitary pad, because apparently people will whisper behind my back.

When you tell me that period stains should be hidden because they are something to be ashamed of, I would shout loud saying that my body is a temple, I am a Goddess.

I have the gift of giving life and will not let you say that I am less.

Let it Bleed

~Anusha Gupta~

Buds blossom into flowers, water evaporates into clouds.
Never have these natural cycles, been questioned by our minds.

But somewhere down the line, a taboo is always found drifting,
Haven't you guessed it yet? Let some fact be unfolded for that.

Monthly it comes, and graciously goes.
Health requires nurturing, just like the plants in spring.
Red pale blood trickles, unstoppable & biological.

Acceptance encourages to cherish every moment,
foster this realistic cycle.
Make an effort to abolish this groundless taboo.

Feel proud to say, yes, I bleed, I bleed!
Because if this exists not, the existence of
homo-sapiens will be a doubt.

For its Time, High Time Now

~Binnie Sharma~

They are emotional, tender and deep, harbor secrets, unexpected to speak.

It saddens me to see superstitions rule our thought, stop raising more walls, this must be fought.

Open your eyes, don't sound so small, for millions still take the fall.

Compounding periods with evil spirits has no logic at all, speak up for yourself, we need to stand tall.

Feel the power and light inside, there is nothing shameful to hide.

We have to break shackles and act with confidence, or others prejudice will be of consequence.

Society takes advantage of your perplexity, why deal with scientific facts with such complexity?

Don't mock linking their mood to when they ovulate, a cold compress or a heating pad would be better.

Let go of ridicule, taboos and restrictions for its time, high time now.

Because Periods Do Not Bring a Period in our Lives

~Deepti Bajaj Khanna~

Jumping, playing, and experiencing the ride.

Curious eyes, vibrant mind.

One day, one wave, pool of blood.

Restrictions come, discrimination hums.

Myths are enforced, presence is ignored.

This question haunts always, why pure blood is called impure, if it bears another soul?

Why periods are made to look like a **period** on all shores?

Why so much hatred, for the artwork of almighty?

What is about this blood that makes everyone so spiky?

This blood is pure, these periods are pure.

It's our pride, there's nothing to hide.

We will jump, we will play, and we will live as if nothing has changed.

We will talk, we will educate those who think it's a shame.

Periods beautify us, periods define us. Because periods do not bring a **period** in our lives.

Vagina Carriers that Bleed every 28 Days

~Dimple Takhtani~

At the ripe age of fourteen,
I found myself questioning religion
sitting all alone on a school bus
parked outside an ancient temple
during a field trip.

I found myself questioning the true intentions
of the educators who asked me
to stay behind because I was on my period.
I wondered how the same teacher who talked about the
dynamic reproductive system in the classroom,
could make me feel out casted for simply having one.

I wondered if the reason India's daughters
were so often victimized
was because we were made to feel ashamed
of possessing the gift of childbirth
from our adolescent years, to them
we were merely walking reminders
of vagina carriers that bled every 28 days.

Red Colored Bliss

~Divya Chatterjee~

You call it a stigma, taboo or a disease,
But menstruation is as simple as the fact that 'we all breathe'

I remember the exam hall which I could not leave,
Kept on bleeding in the seat for 2 hours,
as if my body begged me to freeze...

My skirt was wet and my legs turned red...
The emotions inside me were full of dread...

It was painful not because my belly was in pain,
But for the fact that I could not overcome fear
and all my efforts were in vain...

Back then I did not know that buds are
likely to blossom when the time is right...
Periods is nothing to shy about,
but the darkness of unawareness pleads some light...

Is society actually ashamed of my periods?
Must have took ages of superstition...

When you get a cut on finger and you bleed,
you don't hide it and moan?

Then why there is a different world for me
where I am left to bleed alone?!?

Boycott the myths and praise the beauty of menstruation,
The god you pray to daily, has only given me this divine sensation!

I start my day with the strongest smile that one cannot miss...
Yes, my face glows from nothing but the Red Coloured Bliss!

You, yes You.

~Gaurav Wadhwa~

Hey! Hey! You,
Yes You.
All the beautiful strong people out there,
We are thankful to you.

A phase comes in many human lives
Where they undergo a vaginal blood flow for
days three to five,
It is not a curse please, it's a necessity,
Hold your emotions but show genuine curiosity.

For can you imagine yourself a single day at home?
All alone without your mother?
You would suddenly pray to God,
At least let me once see her.

So, during their age of puberty,
Don't snatch away their liberty.
Let them freely run, jump and play,
Allow them a smooth flight on life's runway.

Let your children be aware of menstruation,
You never know they could be the upcoming sensation.
Menstruation is must at a certain age, it is not filthy,
Hold them, cuddle them and make them relax by showing
them empathy.

And then they will Love You Even More

~Raashi Patel~

Hon, you know who you are.... you're resilient & you love yourself!
You got up before......so, why not might as well this time?

Hey! Listen up!
Embrace yourself, your goals, your body, your beauty,
Coz, why not? and, your chums too!
If they hate them & act weird, then just leave your boo!
Or else you can make them understand, but only if they want to.

Nahh! Don't, just don't do this,
People are toxic & period taboos too!
Embrace the real you, your biology...and then get up & glow up!

No! Don't go there! Nahh! Don't touch this,
Hey you! Stop overreacting & stop being dramatic!
Ughh! I hate this! Don't be ashamed!

And the peeps of the period hate gang, Listen up!
Just upgrade your mentality, why won't you?
You are because your mother bled, your wifey does bleed too!
Nooo, don't push them away, hold them tight & embrace their beauty!

One fine day, your daughters will bleed too!
So, on that day, don't get cringed 'bout it.
Instead, take a step ahead & tell them it's natural & there's nothing wrong w/it!

And then, they will love you even more.

It’s a Different Me

~Radhvi Kapoor~

It's a different world now, or is it a different me?

I don't want to sit down; I want to break free.

They say red is the color of sin, then why do they wear it on their heads.

It's all the beautiful things in the world, which want to change their color to red.

Purest of them all, this blood should be my pride.

For this process is the reason, humankind has spread so wide.

I wonder how they do it, work all day wearing a smile.

Salute to all my heroes out there, I’m joining you all with pride.

Code Red

~Rahul Nayak~

Tell me, "What should I do?"
To my friend, I did the plea.

Stay calm, sit straight, that's what you do,
That's the first call of 'Code Red' for me!

"Periods, it's called", it's a monthly chore.
Said my mom, "Must take care of your".

Did rise the society but on its knee,
That's too much of 'Code Red' for me!

Books I have eaten, a lot to know.
What's this and what's new in the row?

To learn what's hidden in the well,
I cracked the mighty Code Red's spell!

Now, an aura of menstruators surrounded me,
Cheering, wishing to win over the taboo with glee!

Fight's not over, the world must know,
Over the hatred, our positivity must snow!

Preached the truth, for what was right,
Breaking stereotypes, are a treat for sight.

We are breaking the walls with all our might,
'Code Red', we are all with you in this fight!

The fight was tough, swords did clash,
But at the end, the taboo did smash.

Now, it's a gift to embrace.
Every nurturer now says it with grace!

My Encounter with you was so serene,
Out of the Red, we saw the green.

Dear 'Code Red', you stay in the booth,
Biding adieu, it's the human who knew the truth!

A Gentleman Will…

~Shivam Sinha~

The red stain turned them to flowers.

The impurities in your mind have portrayed them impure.

If this is impure, you are impure.

Because you were painted with the same stain when you were born.

A needle of blood donation to save someone's life means great to you.

Then why their monthly blood donation to create a life means less to you.

When they want love, affection and care.

A **gentleman** will make them comfortable in those four days....

Bloody Human

~Shruti Bose~

Yep! That's a Red spot.... behind my white skirt,
Had it been on your fancy tee.... would you still call it a "dirt"?

If it trickles down my thighs. Oh! Then it's a Bane!
Would you still see it with as much disgust.... if it were my bloody vein?

Body becomes exuberantly dynamic all over....my belly weighs like tonnes,
The hormonal surge and the mood swings......I embrace them all at once!

Periods are normal like any natural process.... just like pregnancy or piss,
This pure relationship of Me and my Body....is what I call "The Red Bliss"!

I can wear pads or tampons.... or whatever I want to,
You don't tell me what to choose.... because I own my body and not you!

Nations bleed too but with guns and knives,
Have no shame you strong human.... because we bleed for new lives!

It's hurtful to see people evolving satirically bit-by-bit,
They can use "Period" after a sentence.... but not talk about it!

Let's break this "hush-hush" taboo and all its myths and lies,
Dude, it's the sole cause of your existence.... then why see it with so much despise?

And not all women menstruate.... while some trans-genders do,
And that doesn't make them any "less worthy".... you should know that too!

Just Ask Your Dad

~Samir Kumar Mandal~

Menstruation is ancient alchemy; not a matter of blasphemy.

As explained by her aunts; today, my little girl sees blood in her pants.

Grandma smiles a sigh of relief; she had just turned into a new leaf.

The fruit of knowledge half-eaten by Eve; gift of femininity retrieve.

There are days; when she is PMSing! a rush of emotions and highly intuitive phase;

God save you! if you have done any mess.

After this she turns inward and goes silent, in the cleaning process; all her negative thoughts take a recess.

Then she experiences her energetic best; ready to take new projects, even the most difficult test.

Now she looks and feels more attractive; this is the time, she may say yes, propose now, and don't be proactive.

In some societies, it is a matter of shame, but menstruation does not deserve any blame.

This kind of taboo always leaves a mystery, it cannot be traced in any written record of history.

Don't forget; she is a human with blood, sweat, tears, and emotions, so she must deserve basic sanitation.

Menstrual blood is not impure; it's not a deadly disease that needs a cure.

To keep them in the outhouse with little food and water; this is inhuman and insane.

Protect them; they doesn't need your sympathy or celebration,

Fight for their rights, bleeding ones make a lot of our population.

The transition from Kanya to Kamakhya is normal; we celebrate both, no need to whisper or be formal.

You may follow traditions or choose to roam; it's your wish, charity begins at home.

So, my little child whenever you stained your dress, feeling low or sad; don't worry, need a pad?

Just ask your dad!

Welcome Back, My Dear Mate

~Sonal Wadhwa~

She waits for the menstrual cycle eagerly every month,
Because that makes her feel safe and healthy,
As she now learns more about this phenomenon,
She doesn't like people calling it filthy.

It is during this time that she is most young,
Full of all the energy and vibrancy,
Puberty is the age which makes her attractive,
And she starts to enjoy her adolescence.

She realizes there is no need to be afraid,
She has full rights to breathe in the fresh air.
She now feels like telling the world,
And red now becomes her favourite color.

Taboos such as "you are not allowed to pray"
Do not affect her any more,
It is God who created her like that,
And for everyone equally he keeps open His doors.

To all the beautiful people out there,
I know you all are doing great,
Let us celebrate menstruation together,
And every month say, "Welcome back, my dear date."

Beauty of the Red

~Soumya Sarita Kar~

Your eyes stare unblinkingly when my skirt stains in RED
You scoff at my back, when unaware, I tread.

Your noses turn up at the sight, eyeballs bulge out in shock,
Voices grunt in disgust, and with contempt, my emotions you stroke.

The question arises-Why so shocked!
What's so strange? And, why I'm mocked!

Your daughters giggle at my back as if I'm not one among them,
As if Period is not in their sack, and, the same red puts them in shame!

Your sons tease me, and their eyes bear scorn for I bleed,
Do they hate you (mothers) too! For, we are the same who breed.

You yourself make face at the sight as if I've committed a sin,
Don't you also acknowledge this Godly might? While, to me, you get so mean?

The question arises- Why such ridicule?
What's so strange! And why this red makes you hassle!

Let me ask you- A sort of hatred you bear
For each month I bleed, you think I am quite reed!

Let me convey you-
This very red color brings forth life in you,
Lacking which your mother couldn't have carried you.

Let me enlighten you-
This very RED is the symbol of beauty and health,
Tabooing menstruation you should stop for never does your pride get abashed.

Seeing Red

~Surabhi S Paraki~

What is it about periods that has you seeing red?
That you cannot accept that every month they make the world between their legs their canvas, take it in her hands and paint it red.

You call that blood "impure" as though it wasn't the very blood that made you, or dare I say you've forgotten, that you too were just a single-celled block of unconsciousness, and their wombs breathed life into you and brought you into this world.

You don't see that they carry the seed of life,
Confined to the space between their hips yet, in there, lies the root of the entire human race.

The crimson red in them are like the glowing embers that make their eyes light up, the magenta waterfall flows, and like them, washes everything in its way, a force to be reckoned with.

Their belly houses magic, the sort that gets them through losing enough blood to fill other humans in one lifetime, just to preserve one bloodline.

So, the next time you place their worth to the space in between her legs, or the number of times they've been spread, know that every human was born from it and the world begins and ends the moment they say so.

And the day menstruators decide that they won't spread their legs anymore, the entire world comes to a standstill, and they'll use their blood to place the dot that ends our story, their period will become the full stop.

Reign of the Red Queen

~Uma Hegde~

She flowed that night when
girlhood threw a long, last, look
at the spoils of a short reign,
slipping away to meld melancholy and memories.

Mother who took charge, turning ally,
coached me to wash newly blushing wear.
Once spotless unders of a life gone by,
ushering in a world yet unheard, unfelt, unseen.

She flowed the day I sprinted in the playground,
leaving on my skirt, a flaming, fierce, fleck.
When the loving sisterhood enveloped around;
wrapping my waist with a crisp, crimson cardigan.

Blossoming youth found new meanderings;
springtime tossed dice for life, love, lust.
Ardor cast a glance of promises to fling
And the red cells waited, wisely, welcoming.

Basking in a novel, heady, intimacy,
breath bated, the surreptitiously sliding seed,
headed straight into the red of the sea;
swimming fiercely, claiming cask for creation.

She flowed the morn of a new life,
tugging at my bosom, needy, nifty, kneading.
As I trailed cycles to gage and derive
a steal of magical, memorable, moments.

Eloquent, sage, eyes looked into mine.
affirming the onset of the bloom's blushing bleed.
"Not to worry, mom, I'll be fine."

chimed the confident red riding rookie.

She trickled out one morn as only two drops.
Leaving as she first arrived, benevolently bidding bye.
While uncertainty jostled for room with fear and hopes,
the red queen smiled wry at close of curtain call.

The Lesson of Red

~Yadavi Aggarwal~

Drenched in hatred, that look...
Am I a criminal? My inner being shook.

The marital years were not the same,
Hatred and counters became the game.
The first sweet treatment did not last long,
The Red Bliss was no more a soothing song.

The growing checklist- Hormochange 'n' mood swings,
Womanhood and Procreation, it brings.
Alas! The change in me was condemned,
For I suffered monthly with no end…

Was I diseased, infectious, the symptoms I shown.
Punishment or reward - perplexed with his behaviour unknown.
Indifference and insensitivity- disguised in cold concern,
In loneliness and confusion- those days I burn.

My monthly bliss… leaves me in a fix,
How am I at fault? It pierces me and pricks.
For he loses 'n' misses onto fulfil his lust,
Queer!!! How he vows togetherness till the dust?

Ah! What a facade- your false pride,
Oh! Life partner, I submitted- surrendered, not only tried.

When I bleed, I bleed red,
The colour of love, compassion I shed.
Teach your son this lesson of 'RED',
To fulfil his duty along with earning bread.

Teach him- the monthly cycle- giving life,

Be it our mother, daughter or wife.
Only you can teach him to rever and respect,
To be gentle, caring and celebrate this aspect.

Oh! The biased gender of the ages,
The Red Bliss is my identity,
Not sermon of the sages.

OPEN LETTERS

Love Letter to My Periods

~Priyanka Mohanty~

I LOVE YOU! Sweetheart, hear it one more time! You know that I have never said this to anybody else so many times as much as I have whispered this to you.

I still remember the first time we met. Though our camaraderie has lasted for more than 2 decades now and is still continuing with fervor, I thought let me thank you one more time for what you have done to me.

You have been visiting me 5 days every month and every single time you leave me enthralled with the perfect medley of hormones and transmutation of emotions that you arise in me, which only I could understand. When you arrived, you gave me a chance to look within me and my inner body; while all this time perhaps I was smitten and enraptured only with the exterior self of my body. At the age of 12 you entered my world and metamorphosed it completely. The first drop made me fall in love with my internal body and I realized that menstrual cycle is a sublime phenomenon and a gift from the creator of this world. The chosen ones in this world experience this event and that is when it allows us to spend time honouring our prized bodies. It felt as if I was born again, except that the sounds of celebration were not made public! Blame it on the taboo that existed and perhaps still exists and I fail to understand why. That slight tinge of body ache, those dreamy mood swings, the convolution of energy level, that upsurge in estrogen level, the feel-good chemicals, the craving and munching of dark chocolates, ma's advice to nibble on leafy green spinach, those priceless moments of simply lying down and reading a book or those cherished intervals of nap time – everything that I did while we were together was relish able and welcoming.

I have heard people saying periods are inconvenient, painful, and embarrassing. But sweetheart, why didn't I ever feel that?

I think I know the reason. That's because I never felt that you are an outsider intruding my privacy, rather I welcomed you unopposed and considered you as part of me. Isn't that self-love, the feeling most of us crave for? Then why from times immemorial has history shunned you as sordid and stained and a lot of times has it been petrified of you. Why is there so much of apprehension, dismay, antipathy around you and why are you labelled as a stigma? Periods celebrate fertility, so why aren't we allowed to celebrate? Why is it considered a shame to discuss blood? A research states that there is a considerable percentage of people who still use cloths, rags, hay, ash, and even leaves to manage their periods. There does not seem to be enough awareness around periods.

I know Indian states which celebrate menstruation and I am happy to be born in such a State, Odisha where the three-day festival known as 'Raja Parba' celebrates menstruation each year. I know countries which celebrate menstruation, where menstruators ritually bathe and apply beautiful body paint on the outset of their menstrual cycle, and there are countries which believe that menstruating humans possess greater levels of wisdom and the power to heal while some countries see menstruating people as powerful and sacred.

5 years ago, you took a break and left me for a while only to give me the greatest pleasure of life – Motherhood. You gave me the power to give birth, to be a mother, to bring a life into this world. Those 9 months of holding my baby, those magical and enchanting experiences that my body gave me made me love my body all the more. When you left me, you taught me strengths I never knew existed within me. Again, thank you for gifting me with the power to get a life into this world and I will be ever grateful to you! In fact, I waited for you to come back. People told me that after childbirth, periods will be irregular, accompanied by heavy cramping, spotting might be visible, blood clots might be more evident etc. but happy to say that nothing of this happened and you came back into my life seamlessly like a fairy.

Our love stood strong and you returned the same way you left and did not make me combat an iota of pain or anxiety. Thank you again for that!

I know that one day you will quietly take a pause and completely fade away from my life. I know that those monthly visits of yours will one day cease and soon a day will come when I have to let you go.

And that's when I will miss you. People say there will be hot flushes, internal dryness, mood swings, thinning hair, sleep disturbances and many more aspects but I know that you will take care of it also as you did when you were with me. I know that I will celebrate you when you bid me goodbye just as I have celebrated you when you were with me. I know that there will be a zest and you will take care that as we part ways, we both feel empowered and you shall leave me with a greater sense of confidence and self-possession. We will ring the bell of this illustrious separation together and celebrate this new beginning just as we celebrated with exuberance when you came into my world. I know that you will leave me with self-control, emotional resilience, body acceptance and the ability to be my own self with grace and dignity. I know you want to tell the world not to treat you as a stigma, eradicate the taboo, rather understand, discuss, be proud of you and speak up!

I don't know when we will part ways but at this point in time, I am not eager to say goodbye to you after spending almost a lifetime with you.

And to everybody else – Enjoy the marvel it is while we still have it!

Yours Affectionately

~Prabha Kandhasamy~

Dear Periods,

Even though people look me in an odd way when I menstruate, you will always be something to me. You will always be something special. Right from the day you made your appearance to me till the day you stop, you will always be special.

I have always been not kind to you. Every time you come, I cursed you for all the cramps you gave. I have even gone to the extent of calling you a bitch. I have even cried of why I was born a woman! I have treated you indifferently.

But I wasn't the only one who was treating you indifferently. Every person made me uncomfortable when I menstruated. They treated me differently on those days. They treated me like the way I treat you, "indifferent".

All I ever want is for you to be normalized so that I could be treated as a normal person on those days. But normalizing you involves a peculiar combination of understanding and expressing you.

All the perception people have on you, it's so different and it's a huge world filled with such different perceptions. Maybe I don't know how to change all of their perception on you but I can start by changing mine. Unless the change starts with the individual, there cannot be any change in the society and it is all the society that makes up the world.
Taboos around you should be broken, you should be treated like everything else - "Normal"

A person shouldn't feel insecure every time they get you. And it shouldn't be the responsibility of them alone, but of everyone around them.

So, I have changed my perception on you. Every time you come; I cherish you. People live their lives bound by what they accept as correct and true. And I want everyone to accept you!

Yours affectionately,
All the people who menstruate.

Menstruation, a Gift

~Harshprateek Singh~

Dear reader,

Menstruation is God's gift. With Menstruation females can give birth. According to Science, menstruation, is the discharge of blood tissues from the inner lining of the uterus through the vagina once, every month. Mammals including humans, primates, cattle, horses, some antelopes, giraffes, hippopotamuses, rhinoceroses, elephants, seals, whales, dolphins, and porpoises let foetus develop within their bodies. Thus, they menstruate when their uterus lining does not receive a fertilized zygote to take care of.

Human beings (including all genders) think Menstruation is a curse of the previous life. In this letter that I am addressing everyone, I will use the term 'Menstruator' to depict the inclusiveness of the process and the transformation in the status of those who menstruate in India over the years.

In 4 BC (before Christ) the lady named Mary saw that people were in pain and human life was looking like a curse. Yahoodi was continuously forcing people to adopt the Yahood religion. Mother Mary gave birth to God, "Jesus." But how it was started? It all started with Menstruation. Presently, Christianity is one of the largest religions in the world.

The status of women, as Jawaharlal Nehru says, depicts the social, and mental condition in a nation. Female has been regarded as a symbol of spirituality in our scriptures.

Believing in exactly the same notion, some open-minded citizens like Raja Ram Mohan Roy, Swami Vivekananda, Ishwar Chandra Vidyasagar have shunned off taboos and worked for the upliftment of menstruators and for awakening many societies. Thus, the practices of sati, child marriage, and others were abolished. Various acts such as the Child Marriage

Restraint Act were passed in this direction. Mahatma Gandhi also emphasized on the abolition of child marriages.

Menstruators were also provided training in martial arts. Moreover, they acquired a significant position in politics. Sarojini Naidu was a key figure in this context. She was the first Indian woman to become a President of Indian National Congress and the governor of a state in India. The spread of education and self-consciousness among Menstruators led to their progress over the period. Menstruators of today are empowered and are gaining success in each and every field.

Menstruators today are eager to take up varied professions. Indian women also enjoy equal pay for equal work in comparison to men. There are provisions of both menstrual and maternity leave for them. Furthermore, Menstruators are provided equality of opportunity under Article 16 of the Constitution of India. The Menstruators in urban areas are almost at par in education with the other genders.

The maximum figure of female politicians in the world is from India. They have occupied significant positions i.e., of President, Prime Minister, Speaker of the Lok Sabha, and other high offices. "Indira Gandhi", is the first Female who held the office of the Prime Minister for 15 years.

Remember, Maa Devaki sacrificed her children to end up the evil chapter of Kans, Kauslya Mata gave birth to Prabhu Sri Ram, Mata Anjali gave birth to Sri Hanuman, Mata Tripta Devi gave birth to Sri Guru Nanak Dev.

It all happens due to the process of Menstruation.

Yours Bleedingly

~Ranjitha Ravindran~

Dear Prohibitor,
When I was in Grade 10, I got my first stain. I didn't panic, wasn't even worried. Instead, I looked out for my sister at home and informed her smiling. She shook my hand and said "Wow, congrats!" and then made a call to my mom, with all smiles as if she celebrated me. My mother came home rushing, lifted my hand and said "Well, you must give much care for your health, hereafter". She made me bath, instructed me the ways to use a napkin, and shared her thoughts on personal hygiene and good health. I was made to rest and eat as I wished for the next couple of days. When it got over, I went to school, as always. That is all!

Dear Prohibitor,
How I wish this to happen to every other person out there. It just didn't happen only because of my easy-going mindset, also because of my parents' and siblings' attitude towards menstruation. Just like how you sneeze, how you doze, how you eat, this too happens. Whenever I run out my napkins, my brother would never hesitate to buy me a pack, remembering the exact brand I want. My father would feel how tired I am, and will never hesitate to dispose my napkins stored in the dustbins. I was allowed to consume whatever I wish, go wherever I wish, do whatever I want. Even on the second day, I represented my school basketball team at a district match, when my father stood there, waving hands and cheering for me. My Sister and I, on our periods, were never instructed not to touch anything.

Dear Prohibitor,

No doubt, there are many companies, nowadays, offering "first day period leave" to their employees, along with salary. They do understand menstruation, but don't these men give a backtalk soon after we get back to work, the second day? Their wives didn't take a day off, they think?

Menstruators are still walking miles away to their workplace, having plastic papered napkins between their legs, giving rash on thighs. After travelling for a day, they're pleading the bus drivers to stop the bus at any toilet, to dispose-off their napkins. They still undergo marital-rape even on their first day and shed blood both from their vagina and heart.

Think of those police personnel who would stand all day long at their duty; the nurses who change the patients' napkins, but don't find time to change theirs; that courteous folk at the bill counter who would never get a minute off to have a cup of coffee; your mother who would never stop a moment to take a rest. They are all, on their period.

Dear Prohibitor,
Like how you eat, like how you sleep, like how you urinate, like how you make love, we menstruate. You have any problem with our uterus and ovaries? You stay back, we can't.

Period.

Yours bleedingly,
A Menstruator.

Let's Talk It Out

~Sanjana Kapoor~

Dear reader,

Untouchability, seclusion, discomfort, guilt, social stigma, discrimination.... all these words have become synonymous to menstruation. Silence, hushed up conversations, discomfort...... these are the reactions, we get when we try and talk it out, to anybody regarding it.
My open letter is just an effort to address the shame and taboos that are prevalent in our so-called traditional society regarding periods.

In Hinduism, the colour red symbolizes vitality, power and purity. From weddings to birth of a child and religious ceremonies, red is of utmost significance. The red blood of periods is considered as impure, despite the fact that menstruation marks a person's entry into potential motherhood.

Were myths, taboos and restrictions related to menstruation part of our traditional culture right from the beginning? To this I would say, yes, they were.
We have many traditional families that strictly adhere to myths and taboos related to periods, including seclusion, restrictions on physical mobility, forbidden entry at religious places and kitchen and even barring the use of sanitary napkins due to notion that it might affect the menstruator's ability to conceive, forcing to use dirty rags owning to the cost related to sanitary napkins.

Banishment/ disbarment is prevalent in Gond, one of the largest tribal groups in India. They spread over the states of Eastern Maharashtra, Chhattisgarh, Uttar Pradesh, Andhra Pradesh, Bihar, Madhya Pradesh and Odisha. In these parts, menstruators are considered as untouchable, during their monthly cycles. They are made to make through their periods in isolation.

They are sent to live in basic huts made outside the villages for the purpose. The thatched huts, are public properties, and no one takes the responsibility for their upkeep. They are poorly made, and, lack basic amenities. Even the bathrooms are made using bamboos. These huts don't have a kitchen, and those staying inside have to rely on a family member for food and other essential items. They're made to sleep on the floor. The huts are usually located on the edge of forests, and it is common for wild animals to enter in. Many die owning to snake bites and a few of them also suffer sexual harassment by the locals. These places lack proper sanitation owing to which they become susceptible of developing dysuria and genital itching. Confined spaces, feeling of left out; create an environment of extreme vulnerability.... these conditions put some serious impact on mental well-being of menstruators, especially, adolescents who have just taken their first step to puberty.

The way menstruation products, are advertised in India, has a lot to do with, how the society takes it. Earlier, the ads were just made to sell the products. They didn't play any part to eradicate the stigmas attached to it.
I still remember the whisper ad of 2014. A girl is sitting and worrying about her hockey match. Her mother comes into the picture and gives her new whisper sanitary napkin. There was no conversation between the two regarding the periods. It was considered obvious that if a girl is stressed out that would be because of menstruation.

The ad's protagonist didn't even talked about periods. They referred to them as 'mahina' or 'un dino'. The white backgrounds used in the commercials, clearly show the desperation to eliminate any sign or mark that makes evident that women are bleeding.

However, the newer commercials are really ground breaking in their approach. But there is still more the media can do to completely eradicate the myths and stigmas attached to periods.

Let's start the change from our homes. Someone has to take a strong lead, be it a mother, father or son. When a mother teaches her daughter about monthly cycles, make sons the part of it too. It's also important for a society to have sensitive men. All genders should understand the relevance of menstruation. Don't make it only the women's world. Let fathers be the part of it too.

I know, in India, people live in joint families and sometimes it is very difficult to convince an old member of the family, but one step at a time, may ease the path and slowly and gradually the discrimination might stop.

Mothers do it for your daughters; sons do it for your sisters, friends and to-be-wives; and fathers, stand up for once and you will see the change it brings. Next time, any one from your family is menstruating, help them. Don't wrap the sanitary napkin under your sleeve, take it openly. Don't be ashamed about it. Carry it confidently. It's what completes you. Schools please don't be the part of herd mentality. Impart knowledge to both boys and girls regarding it. So that the next time, someone stains red, no one mocks or teases, but supports.

Communication Matters

~Sonali Mandal~

Dear mothers,
Talking about personal subjects like periods or menstruation can make you and your kid a little uncomfortable. But if you can show little guts (especially in a traditional Indian society), it certainly can help your kids understand and respect their bodies. Trust me, just like we care about proper nutrition, the best education and strive to instil the right value system in them, talking about bodies (life processes) will solve tons of issues in their growing up years. This will help them make good decisions about their health and hygiene. After all, "Health is wealth".

When is the right time to talk with your kids about periods?

It should not be one 'big talk' or 'blood secret' you ask your daughter to keep when she gets her first period. Rather, you must slowly build your child's understanding of bodily functions, let them explore their own bodies.

Please don't hesitate to talk to your sons too! As tomorrow he is going to be the husband, the father, the teacher, the shopkeeper, the colleague or the co-worker, etc.

When your 'boy' turns into a 'man', our thinking around menstruation would have changed – it would just be a 'non-event'

– a body function, that happens majorly with women, and that's it. Nothing more, nothing less. We would not have to write open letters anymore, he would not have to talk about it as a separate subject, he would not have to participate in discussions on the social and cultural change regarding periods.

Both girls and boys need reliable information about periods. Never ignore the fact that even transgender menstruate.

- For example, you should not hurriedly remove the packet of sanitary pads from your grocery bag lest your 4-year-old child asks what it's used for. Encourage them to ask all sorts of questions. You can simply explain to them, "Women bleed a little from their vagina every month. It's called a period. It isn't because they are hurt. That's how our body gets ready for a baby. The sanitary pads soak the blood so it doesn't spoil our dress."

Over the years you can give your child more information as they grow up. Now that you have already given them the basic idea.

In a different scenario, if your child doesn't ask questions about periods, you can bring it up by the time they are 6 or 7 years old, by this age most kids can understand the basics of periods. Look for a natural moment to talk about it. Never should it be a 'closed doors affair' for it unknowingly affects your child's psychology, they can perceive menstruation to be secretive or dirty, "unclean thing". You can share the basic information.

- For example, as a girl develops into a woman her body changes so she can have a baby when she grows up. A part of that is getting a place ready for the baby to grow inside the mom. The place where the baby grows is called the uterus. Every month the uterus walls get ready for a baby. If there is no baby the uterus wall sheds off and bleeds a little. The blood comes out of a woman's body through the vagina. The body makes a new wall every month in case there is a baby.

Many mothers don't feel comfortable speaking about their normal, healthy, bodily functions with their sons. If they don't educate their sons, how do they expect them to hold an informed conversation with any woman- their future girlfriends and wives? No wonder so many women find out that their husbands have no clue what period is, till they learn it from them!

Communication is the key, it's important for girls to be able to talk to their dad, brother or whoever for that matter. So that they're properly cared for.

Gosssh! Men and Periods?

~Tanmay Anand~

Dear menstruators,

Just let's take a moment and think why we - the society have not been able to normalize periods. The root cause of this problem is that we are the prisoners of our own thoughts and culture.

It's not that I am the first person writing about it. Many people have come forward to normalize it, but they were suppressed by the society and their so-called valuable ethics.
When the whole world is developing, new technologies are being invented, entrepreneurs are in full enthusiasm - there we are, just a handful, trying to just eradicate the taboo associated with different aspects of life through our writing. It's high time that we talk about it openly with everyone - yes everyone including the men too.

Ghoshhh! Men and Periods?

To most of us it would just look like the most unpleasant combination in this world. To some the most un-relatable words in this world or to some like the two parallel lines which can never intersect. But interestingly today I am going to talk about this topic only - MEN AND THE PERIODS. Personally, I am just sick of listening that men will be men. We as a society fail because most of the time we just act like sexists. Although such a category of men might be rare or rarest of rare, but we have to believe that such men exist, there are so many men working with different organizations for women's rights, for sexual abuse cases and for periods as well. When a random man just tells me that there's stain on my pants and I should just check my pants. The first thought that comes to my mind is that he is a pervert, without thinking that he might genuinely be telling me this.

Although I too have experienced how it feels when a group of boys just mock at you for that red stain. But again, these are those who do not respect god because He is the one who created our wonderful body and its processes. Because of such men and what we have been taught from childhood only we women have become much more conserved about it than it is required. We too are now not ready to accept that periods are normal and we can openly talk about this to anyone around us. There is nothing to feel ashamed of.

We can discuss about this in front of the boys. We can buy sanitary napkins as easily as we buy our daily essentials. We can ask the men around us about the stain on our pants. One quality of the men around us that we should try to inculcate is that boys are very open about their sexual pleasures or periods and are willing to normalize it. But it is now we the women who choose to remain silent. And it is absolutely normal because we live in the country where most of the rapes and sexual abuses occur. What I am trying to say is that we should ourselves try and talk about it with boys too - not with every guy but with our family members and our friends at least.

Rather than just blaming the society, we should just come forward, stand on a hilltop and yell 'We bleed, yes we bleed to carry your bloody generation forward. My uterus just gets ready every month to carry a beautiful life in it. And we are proud that God gifted us this power to bring and nurture a new life to this earth. We are thankful that God made us this strong to carry two lives at the same time."

Eradicating Menstruation Taboos

~Simran Chauhan~

Dear Google Generation, I am talking about Men/suration, rather it should be called Life/suration! Goodness me! LOL!

We, are a generation trying to normalize this word or I should say trying to normalize fear/uneasiness/doubts associated with this word which has been twisted by myths and passed on to us by previous centuries just like many other things.

This question always comes in the mind of any teenager when they just enters into this "Life Givers' Club" that what does mensuration have to do with purity, God, worshiping places, rituals, entering kitchen, washing hair, bathing etc. as it is just haemoglobin coming out of a body part which further is just a functional processor of this life-giving club?

The flood of questions continues in their mind when they are told to hide sanitary pads, are scolded if "Whisper" or "Stayfree" comes out of their mouth in front of any man or in public. They observe that these words spread uneasiness in the air as if they said something in respect of criminal offence or have disrespected someone.

First few years of 21st century were not Google years hence till then living with those questions and passing them to new generation was justified due to lack of knowledge. But today we "THE GOOGLE GENERATION" depend on internet for quenching almost every thirst of knowledge, so living with mensuration taboos today is just not justified. You have to find answers to those questions in your mind now!

Myth 1: Washing hair/ bathing in warm water during mensuration is a bad omen and can stop your blood flow and further affect your fertility later in life.

Fact: This myth is just an old wives' tale which may have started during ancient times when people used to go to lakes, rivers for bringing drinking water and for household chores. These water bodies were public places, so bathing there would have brought unpleasant feelings for others or contaminate the lake with blood as the water body was also the source of drinking water.

There is no connection between washing hair with bad omen. This myth may also have started as washing hair may drain your energy in those days and should be avoided (in reference to many historical studies). No study demonstrates that hair washing during periods cause any kind of disease.

Moreover, it is very important to maintain your personal hygiene (by bathing, showering, shampooing your head). Also, skipping bath in those days can lead to reproductive tract infections.

Myth 2: Do not visit temples, touch godly things, and worship during your periods

Fact: Mensuration is viewed differently across globe due to variety of cultures. In some historic cultures, menstruating women were considered as sacred, pure and powerful which was viewed as a danger to men's power. Hence, when women's blood was considered sacred and powerful, the society ritually set women apart.

There are many taboos regarding mensuration with which we are living today and which can't be covered in an article.

But what can be covered is idea of not believing in the stories which are passed on to us from previous generations. Don't occupy your thoughts with my writings too, just search yourself, interrogate your thoughts, engulf yourself with knowledge and then decide what you want to pass on- Taboos or Self-Love?

Dear Nani, Dadi, Mami, Chachi. etc

~Supriya Omi~

Dear Dadi, Nani, Mami, Chachi etc,

Needless to say, there might be something wrong with the notion that you have in your mind regarding "Menstruation" that has made me come here and address you personally. Over years we have been subjected to this unethical and stereotypical mentality. But why such biases? Aren't you as well gifted with the same thing?

Over years you have been telling us that a menstruating person should be kept safely and away from coming in the eyes of others, as if we are some vault! You have also been going around making judgments on people who have issues in this part of their lives. The best part is that more than half of you treat us indifferently when you come to know that we have hit our menstrual cycle. How ironic?

"Don't touch this! Don't sit there! Don't eat this! Don't wear this!"

"How can you go around saying that you are on your periods? Shame!"

Really! Is it a matter of shame?

Isn't it something that we must be really proud of? There is a reason that we have been blessed with something like this. The amount of pain a female body can bear during the labor is insane. The ones who have gone through it, know about it pretty well. You too have young folks in your house who bleed. You are well aware of the facts and ideas behind menstruation.

You make us believe as if we are committing some crime by menstruating. Let me put it well and clear. It is just another part of a life process. If you ask any biology student, they would tell you how simple it is. After we hit our puberty, every month our ovary releases an egg (the female reproductive cell). This egg cell has a tendency to get fertilized by the sperm (male reproductive cell). Since the whole biological female reproductive system anticipates this fertilization, various other changes also occur in the other organs of their body. On failure of getting fertilized, this egg cell along with some other ruptured blood vessels is thrown out of the body. That's what you call menstrual bleeding. Simple and clear.

I clearly didn't feel anything wrong or absurd about it. It's just another simple process like digestion, apart from the fact that different body parts are involved. Then why are there so many taboos and stigmas related to it? Surprisingly, over years a small part of the male section of the society could understand this simple process and the best part is that they are supportive. Do you even understand how mundane it is for them? But still our fathers, brothers and lovers are far more accommodating with this simple process than you are. Ironic!

You should teach us to be more comfortable in talking about this rather than being shameful. There is a reason there are so many youngsters and elders alike going through many menstrual disorders and still don't speak up. Funnily, even doctors are more concerned about "life choices" rather than taking the actual matter into consideration. You as mothers, sisters, grandmothers, aunts and friends should come ahead and take this matter into consideration. Be our inspiration and make us fall in the love with our womanhood. The idea is not to let you feel down but instil a new outlook in your minds.

Regards,

A girl whose father is more woke about menstruation than other members of the family.

Menstruation, What is it?

~Riya Gupta~

Menstruation has become a hot topic and everyone is talking about it. How it is normal, how it's not something impure, period memes and the list goes on.

Do we know what it is? People who say a women bleeding, menstruating, is impure do they know what it is?

Let's understand it, the female reproductive organ consists of ovaries (an organ which protects the eggs stored, release the eggs and secretes hormones such as estrogen, progesterone etc.) which starts producing ova or egg (female reproductive cell) after puberty, after the egg is released, it passes through a tube called fallopian tube, where fertilization occurs if the sperm (male reproductive cell) fuses with the egg. The cycle results in formation of the lining of the uterus (required for pregnancy to support the child), but when the egg is not fertilised the lining is released along with the unfertilized egg, which causes blood. The flow of blood from the uterus is known as menstruation or a "period".
So, the question is, is it impure? Yes, if our existence is. Which is certainly not considered as impure.

Now let's understand the restrictions around menstruation.
Don't cook food!
Don't go to the temples!
Don't exercise!

Essentially all these restrictions involve 'movement'. So, the idea behind them is to encourage people on their period to relax.

Why not temples?

Think! What sanitation facilities were there back then? So how would it be to roam around while you are bleeding, that too without any bandages? This is just one aspect. How was the habitat? Were animals who can smell blood far off? There are many more reasons.

Why not to exercise or do yoga?

Yoga, essentially, we talk about hatha yoga. The hatha yoga, especially asanas which involve twisting body in various forms are restricted for menstruators while on their period.

While you must not perform certain asanas, there are some you can, such as tadasan, triyak tadasan, kati chakrasan etc.

Also, one can also practice pranayam such as anulom vilom, sheetli etc.

Do you know that menstruation increases the awareness and sensitivity? It is considered as the best time for a person to meditate.

Understand your body, your cycles, what you should eat, exercise, and then there will be no taboo, only knowledge and beauty.

Beauty of Menstruation

~Dr. Smita Todkar~

Dear people working in the field of Menstruation, Sexual and Reproductive Health,

Ayurveda recognizes that menstruation is a physiological process. The four phases of the menstrual cycle happen periodically in female biology. Due to them they are blessed with holding their own progeny. In ancient times there was no availability of calendars, so the moon's shape and days between '*Full moon day*' and '*New moon day*' were the measuring calendar. And that's why the normal period cycle (in majority) was calculated as 28 days. Also, as we all know the definition according to science in this modern era says the same and the period of 22 to 35 days is considered normal. But it can vary in some. That is the beauty of menstruation, it's different yet a similar experience for every menstruator. *"स्त्यायतीअस्या गर्भा इति स्त्री I"* (Styayatiy asmat garbha iti stree) means 'a body which holds uterus and fetus is known as female body'. The definition of a biological female body in Ayurveda explains the beauty of menstruation. Apart from holding the fetus, the uterus needs to bleed at regular intervals, after the attainment of menarche (starting of menstruation). If any biological female hasn't attained menarche (in Ayurveda, it's called '*hrutu*') then she's unable become a biological mother.

This is first phase of menstruation in which we are able to see the bleeding externally, but the other three phases (pre-ovulatory/ follicular, ovulatory/ovulation and post-ovulatory/ luteal) occur completely inside the body. Except during the periods of pregnancy, lactation, and the physiological attainment of menopause (stoppage of Menstruation). This means that from menarche to menopause a person can menstruate 360 times. Each of the ovaries alternatively produces eggs these many times. This is an amazing calculation and coordination within our own bodies.

Through this we get to learn how we can *'try and try, again and again, without being tired'*, and its mere physiology, maintaining the basic body functions. Definitely sometimes we have to face few problems like pain, excess bleeding, irregularity etc. but that's another way of our body signaling us, for providing more care towards it. Such thing happens as our lifestyle is changing and so many times, we are bombarding our body with unnecessary things, may be food, and may be external environment.

Working as a public health professional with different communities including rural and tribal populations, I got to understand how the scenario related to menstruation changes. Menstruation isn't only related to how anyone manages it or what absorbent material they use. But unfortunately market driven products ask us to only think about that. Even in the National Family Health Survey (NFHS) 4 (2015-2016) India fact sheet, the definition of hygienic methods of protection during the menstrual period is pre-decided as, 'Menstruators who used locally prepared napkins, sanitary napkins or tampons during their menstrual period.' This is painful, being a public health researcher in the area of menstruation and adolescent health. To add on, the disposal of sanitary napkins is a huge challenge in front of us, especially in a country like India. The guidelines under Rashtriy Kishor Swasthya Karyakram (RKSK) say, the inclusion of a working incinerator for each and every school, but no data is available about its availability. The local schools in rural areas and tribal areas don't even have it.

Our duty is to keep the earth in its natural course and vibrant ecological system in a balanced condition. We are failing already, but due to this pandemic the healing capacity of earth is realized again. This has so much resemblance to the female biology. Menstruation has a similar role in a body's healing. So, we are capable enough to celebrate this healing process for ourselves and thanking nature by shifting ourselves towards sustainable absorbent products, by keeping our greed aside.

According to published research '*Rajaswala Paricharya: Effect on Menstrual cycle and Its associated symptoms*', the intervention proves an effective result with problematic menstruation, just by following the code of conduct as mentioned in the texts of Ayurveda. Nowadays we have also rediscovered "*Yoga and Aasanas*" for curing or getting relief from menstrual problems.

New Zealand made menstrual absorbents freely available for all school children in the country. Similarly, by many organizations are a day off during menstruation is declared for menstruators. These are the policies and steps showing the beginning of new era, era of "The *Beauty of Menstruation*". I hope we will keep all these things in mind and cherish 'menstruation' just as 'menstruation'.........

Period Positivity

~Swati Kansra~

In India, the term mensuration has several social, religious, cultural and femininity inferences. The prohibitions and stigma that rotates around mensuration run into wrong explanations, deceptive beliefs, lack of educational discussions on menstrual and reproductive health, and chief ambiguities in accessibility and awareness about menstrual hygiene. The present generation receives the immoral knowledge and myths about this taboo and passes it from one person to another.

I am writing this letter to highlight the importance of menstruation and to highlight the changing new waves in menstruation which have been instrumental in fostering period positivity. In conventional days, buying of menstrual supplies such as tampons and pads were taken as the coil of shame and they were hidden away from curious eyes of the community. However, there is a swing, as more and more people and campaigners alike show us why mensuration is a feeling of pride rather than a symbol of shame. Therefore, we must talk frankly, loudly and proudly for the assistance of all menstruators around the world.

My dear reader, being period positive is to open up to relearning and understanding menstruation. If we can share our feelings, emotions and blemishes to the society then why do we feel humiliation while talking about the natural bodily process such as mensuration?

Many mensurators have been making headlines either on social media and newspapers by exposing to the world that there's nothing dirty when mensuration period comes. Moreover, it is being period positive to say 'menstrual' products instead of 'sanitary products', because periods are not a stigma for the society.

People are coming forward to spread awareness about sustainable alternatives to menstrual sanitation. Sustainable mensuration refers to utilizing environment-friendly substitutions to single-use, non-biodegradable menstrual products like cloth pads, menstrual cups, biodegradable sanitary pads, period panties to condense the left-over created by non-biodegradable ones. In India, there are several places where manual scavenging, waste picking and seclusion is done by hand. A sustainable method towards menstruation also endeavors to hold the issue of human rights and dignity of manual scavengers. In India almost 6% of non-ecological waste is created by sterility products including mensuration products, wipes and diapers.

It is period positivism and inclusiveness for people of every class, age, gender, race or culture to communicate about mensuration and for everybody to comprehend those who are on the verges and who are influenced inter-sectionally in this discourse. It should not be assumed as shameful or be elevated as a contender of womanhood. It is just a biological process rather than any communal norm.

Even the menstrual time of a month is not just preventative but it reveals tons of information about your body functioning. For instance, being overweight, underweight and having extreme stress might prevent your period arriving time and if you get regular periods then it indicates the sign that all key areas like your hormones and associated organs are working effectively.

Sometimes a person's cycles are irregular, which means they come at a different time every month. This might happen due to pregnancy, excessive stress, approaching menopause, vigorous exercise, hormone disorders and associated problems like endometriosis and PCOS. One must take note of any changes in color and consistency and it is always wise to discuss changes in mensuration with the doctor.

There's a cultural, social and gendered gist affixed to menstruation. All glorify the elemental nature of women i.e., to reproduce, they think about them as destructive when women don't menstruate or breed for several reasons. The ability of the women to procreate and menstruate has got nothing to do with her inclination either to have a child or not.

However, media plays an indispensable role in spreading positivity towards menstruation. Our superstars and other TV actors are doing numerous shows and advertisement campaigns to awake people about this natural phenomenon. Many educational and NGO platforms are becoming conscious and organizing seminars, fundraisers and activities to alter the thinking of present generation and cease its stigma from the mind of each youngster.

These days, periods are being discussed unashamedly in our political and cultural institutions, but we need to make sure that is also happening in our day-to-day life discussion. All genders of the present generation need to be taught about periods and the beauty of the process needs to be realized fluidly by all gender identities.

KNOW THE AUTHORS

Sapna Jadhav Eldandi

Sapna is a writer and an avid storyteller from the city of dreams... Mumbai. She discovered a passion for writing after graduating with a Masters in English Literature and she dove into the world of teaching and still continues to inspire young minds. Her stories manifest life with all its unexpected twists and turns.
Her popular published compositions include Eternally with Him, Harmony Conquers, Make Up, Window seat, Hopefully Soon and Smiling Waves.

In her free time, Sapna loves to travel with her close-knit friends. Music and coffee are her partners. Blogger, scriptwriter and a storyteller, she is a plethora of multifaceted talent.
She strongly believes in taking life as it comes. Her charisma and undeniable charm would certainly inspire anyone to grab a pen and unleash the writer in them.

Smriti Sharma

Being an avid reader, writing has always been something Smriti wanted to do since a long time.

Fabricating stories out of every day mundane life and pouring out magic has always driven her to write more.
One day she wishes to publish her own book.

Snover Sanduja

A 21-year-old, day dreamer who wishes to bring change in the world by doing one good dead at a time, Snover sought serenity in writing and believes that the strength under the tip of her pen is greater than mere spoken words. She writes with an aim to knock the doors of our society and open as many blindfolds as possible.

Life has never been honey and sugar but she has always believed in 3 L's - Live, Learn and Love.
According to her, she is no perfectionist but she grabs every opportunity in order to learn.

Chloe

Chloe, student and resident in the state of Illinois, loves to share her love towards humanity through her writing. She is excited to continue studying and further her skills in the future universities she will attend.

She has always been thankful towards God and the wonderful family she is blessed with, furthermore she says she'd like to thank the inspiring women who have made an impact on her life.

Priyanka Chugh

Born and bought up in city of Gurus, Priyanka Chugh is a professor, social worker, event organizer, and co–author of 4 books.

With a teaching experience of more than 8 years, she has always been an active member of the NSS and also volunteers for various NGOs dedicated to the society and protection of the environment. She takes a keen interest in writing poems, research papers and short stories.

Navneet Singh Bal

Navneet is a 21-year-old student pursuing Social Sciences, he has been volunteering for an organization to normalize periods among rural areas and also happens to be an active part of an open learning space.

His interests include human behavior, arts and cultures and he aspires to work in these fields. He is an avid reader and nature lover who always loves to explore new things and perspectives in life.

Sonali Mandal

Sonali Mandal is a parent of a teenage son and a homemaker. She stayed in many parts of the country, courtesy of her father and husband. This experience helped her to grow as an honest, open-minded, and generous individual.

She is a science graduate with a B.Ed. degree and worked as a PRT in different schools for about 12 years, besides working as a part-time abacus instructor for a year. She was an active NSS volunteer and worked on field for women and children's health.

She loves to participate in various writing contests to express herself.

Shatabdi Manna

Shatabdi Manna has completed post-graduation in English and Comparative Indian Literature from University of Delhi. She is currently working as a project assistant at the Indira Gandhi National Centre for the Arts (IGNCA), New Delhi.

She is fascinated with stories that are always around us in some or the other form. This is her first attempt at short-story writing and these stories are dedicated to the feelings of support and care that lie within all of us.

Her interest lies in stories, music, cinema, food and travel. She occasionally writes poems and aspires to create good and engaging tales to tell.

Sonal Wadhwa

Sonal Wadhwa is an ERP Consultant by profession and has performed audits for Fortune 500 companies. Alongside, she is working on her own Direct Selling Business and is an upcoming author of a book revolving around the importance or building multiple sources of income.

She has an innate interest in writing poetry, short stories, articles and posts for social media marketing. She strongly believes that women are self-empowered individuals and given a chance, can prove out to be best leaders in their fields.
She wants to break stigmas around menstruation and that led her to raise her opinions around the same.

Soumya Sarita Kar

Soumya Sarita Kar resides in Cuttack, Odisha and originally hails from Kendrapara, a coastal district of Odisha.
She is an M.A. and an M.Phil. in English Literature. She can read, write and speak Odia, Hindi, English and amazingly, French as well.
Her passion for literature inspires her to try her hand at poetry and short stories. One of her short stories has already been published in an anthology titled 'Cryptic Encounters.'

Vanshika Seth

Vanshika is a 20 years old individual making small contributions towards bringing a big change in this world and according to her, writing and speaking about menstruation is a part of that change.

Her aim is to see a world where people can openly talk about periods, where a pad is no longer wrapped in a black polythene, where boys and girls are given equal understanding of the process at school level, where having a stain is no longer a shame for society.
She strives to make this world a better place to live.

Adya Gupta

Adya says she has been writing since forever and is someone who definitely finds joy in the art of writing.
She never thought that something which was a way of expressing her emotions would get her published someday!
She'd like for the world to be a better place where everyone is just a little more kind to each other.

Kumari Anusha Gupta

Kumari Anusha Gupta is a B. Com Hons. graduate from Delhi University and is also pursuing a professional degree alongside.

Being a creative child since school itself, she loved to read articles and poems on different social causes and the environment, this helped her develop her interest in writing.

She believes words are the perfect way to convey thoughts and pave way for new one's.

Binnie Sharma

Binnie Sharma is an Assistant Professor in Commerce and Business Administration. She is also pursuing her PhD from Guru Nanak Dev University, Amritsar.

Her areas of expertise include Services Marketing, HRM and Entrepreneurship. She has a teaching experience of 15 years.

An avid reader and daydreamer, she believes in growth through balance and positivity.

Deepti Bajaj Khanna

Recent writer turned poet with a penchant for all things adventurous, Deepti writes for the heart from the heart.

A product designer by profession, and a wild child at heart, creativity fuels her desire to explore, experience and create.

In a world that is constantly trying to drown out real, authentic, raw feelings, she strives to make her authentic voice heard in her words, with her curiosity and by sheer existence.

Dimple Takhtani

Dimple is a 24-year-old amateur poet. She writes free verse poetry about her personal experiences of living away from home, existentialism, LGBTQ representation and anything that intrigues or enrages her.

She has been published by various digital publications such as Bloom, Visio Mag, Brown Girl Mag, In plain speak among others.

Divya Chatterjee

Divya is a Chartered Accountant by profession and currently working with Credit Suisse at Pune. Contrary to her profession, she is an art inclined person who loves to find joy in everything and loves to express her feelings with poetry most of the times. One can find doodling lines in almost every notebook she uses and says it is amusing how every time one can get to know themselves better when they read their own poetry.

Being an organizer and volunteer for many social welfare events now, she firmly says that true happiness can only be found in making others happy. She's also been titled as 'The Best Leader' and 'The Best Volunteer' by the renowned NGO- 'Being Social'.

Another thing which is food to her soul is dancing and she is currently trying her hands ('feet' would be more appropriate) on Latin dance forms. She finds bliss in laughing hard with family and friends.

Gaurav Wadhwa

Gaurav Wadhwa was born and brought up in Meerut, studied in Dehradun and worked in Ghana, West Africa. He is a Chemical Engineer by profession and a poet by rhyme who spends his idle time cooking and travelling.

He claims to be a patient person and the sense of keeping calm in difficult situations always works best to his advantage, he says.

Raashi Patel

Raashi is an 18-year-old student pursuing Business Management.

She is passionate about art and writing, loves fashion, travelling, fitness, watching movies and cannot leave out shopping, she says.

She dreams to have her own fashion and skincare brand in the future.

Radhvi Kapoor

Radhvi is a writer and blogger pursuing her bachelor's degree in Psychology. Been writing from 4 years, she has created fictional stories, poems, quotes, and tries to help people deal with their emotions through her introspection series.

An unusual soul who loves to read and heal people, she takes pride in calling herself a part time philosopher who is constantly juggling between reality and imagination.

Rahul Nayak

Rahul, a student who is currently pursuing his Bachelor Degree loves writing stories. He started writing about 4 years ago and is currently working on his debut novel.

He has an eminent appetite for movies and hence, his works are a visual treat in themselves. He says, "Romance exists in every element, you just need an eye to see it!"

Shivam

Shivam hails from Gaya, a town in Bihar and is currently pursuing B. Tech from Nagpur. Writing is his way of expressing.

He has been wanting to show the world the power of Vedic Sciences and to derive logic using it.

Apart from painting, cricket, technical writing, he loves to listen to the screams of night sky which calls out to explore the hidden cosmos.

Shruti Bose

Shruti from Chandigarh, is an MBBS student and has a passionate inclination towards writing poems which mainly stress the issues of the modern contemporary society.

She possesses a dexterous skill of making sketches and portraits. She says it's equally important to be aware of menstrual hygiene and STDs as much as it is to normalize menstruation for a healthier society.

As a medical student, she makes it a point to actively contribute in raising awareness about menstrual health.

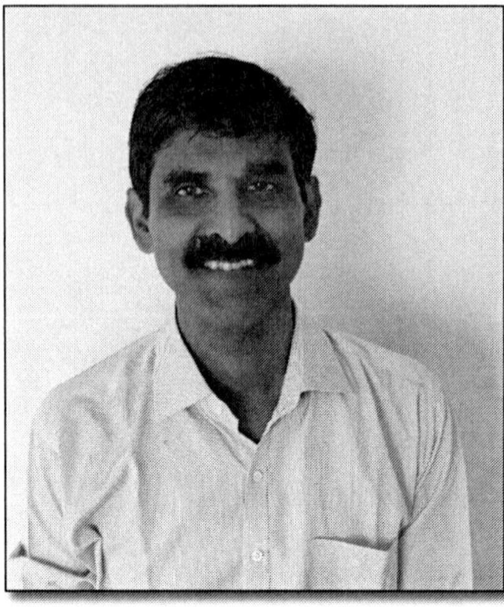

Samir Kumar Mandal

Samir Kumar Mandal has been working as a textile engineer for the last 25 years. He was born and brought up with the ideas and ideals of Tagore and Vivekananda and likes to explore the intricacies and nuances of human relations.

He is a strong votary of woman empowerment. Though he is a forward-looking man, he likes to see any incident in hindsight.

Surabhi S. Paraki

Surabhi is a curious mind with a love for poetry and loves animals more than humans.

She happens to be an ardent feminist who is looking forward to a revolution in gender equality, and a strong ally of the LGBTQ+ community.

She is also an RCBian and proud of it.

Uma Hegde

Uma Hegde is a technical writer living in Bangalore. She has been writing since the age of 9, mostly for herself and her family. Her writing skills were recognized early by her dad who roped in her services to communicate with his clients.

She has a son and 2 daughters. Period positivity resonates completely with her having always imparted the right values and understanding of it to all her children.

She is passionate about reading, music, and loves travelling, a trait she shares with her husband. Her wish is to write her grandmother's story, someday.

Yadavi Aggarwal

Yadavi Aggarwal is a 19-year-old young enthusiast who wants to capture the world with her creative and artistic skills in various genres of life.

She has recently started sharing her poems with the world and she is equally devoted to transforming the simple homely looks into stunning glamorous ones that catch the attention of even the cold eyed. As a makeup artist she adds beauty to faces and spreads smile on the beholder's face.

Yadavi looks beyond the usual definition of success, name and fame but seeks to have her own edge by creating or doing for her self-satisfaction thus sustaining the essence of every Art.

Dedicated to her dreams (she has many), she is passionate and resolute to fulfill all gradually along with her academics.

Priyanka Mohanty

Priyanka Mohanty is an experienced global HR professional in the area of 'Talent Management & Engagement, apart from being a 'Global Diversity & Inclusion' champion.

She has been conferred with 'Woman HR Leader of the Year' by BW Business world, 'Women Achievers Award in Corporate Sector' by ASSOCHAM, 'HR 40under40' by Jombay to identify India's top 40 young HR Leaders, '101 HR Super Achievers' by World HRD Congress and many more.

She is a Chemical Engineer who chose to pursue her passion in HR. She is extremely passionate about writing and is a published author in multiple print and digital platforms.

Prabha Kandhasamy

Prabha is a budding rookie, slowly crafting her way into this amazing world of literature. As an aspiring writer, she says she has always wondered that words have immaculate power to change the outlook of one's perspective. This in turn has glided her passion towards this art form.

Her message to all the readers out there is to follow their passion, live their dream and see themselves fly like the child inside them.

Harshprateek Singh

Harshprateek has always thought for the betterment of society. He runs an NGO named 'Education Planet Welfare Society' for uplifting needy children.

He actively participates in various social activities aimed at a harmonious society by spreading education and health awareness. He is a social activist, writer, YouTuber, and an entrepreneur.

Ranjitha Ravindran

Ranjitha Ravindran, is a freelance copywriter and a voice over artist. Her love for words made her pen several short stories, blogs & poems. She has published her own e-book, which is an anthology of poems.

She is also a biker and an avid traveler who wants to be a digital nomad with her dog aside. Yeah, one life live it queen size!

Sanjana Kapoor

Sanjana Kapoor is a content writer by profession who has been working in the field for more than seven years with writing being not only her profession but passion too. It all started when her best friend moved out of the city, and she penned down first letter to her; pouring her heart out to her.

From letter to friends, to letter to editors, article writing, blogging... she just loves every bit of it. She holds a Masters' degree in Journalism, from BBK DAV College, Amritsar. Currently, she lives in London with her husband and a five-year-old son.

Tanmay Anand

Tanmay Anand is a girl with strong opinions. Along with raising concerns over the issues prevailing in the society she often writes love through her poetry and prose both in English and Hindi languages.

She is a budding writer and a student of Medical Sciences. She is an active member of a few writing pages on social media and is currently working with a student-based volunteer organization and raising awareness against child sexual abuse.

She tries to find happiness in the little moments that life offers. A dog lover at heart she believes that no one can be a better teacher than nature in the subject of love and harmony.

Simran Chauhan

Simran Chauhan is an engineer and works as a Business Analyst in Tata Consultancy services. She is a published poet and writer and calls her a consistent learner. She has a constant inclination towards art.

She founded 'Being Motichoor' which is a fund-raising organization in the city of Amritsar and has been responsible for organizing many charity events in the city.

She is also an active performer and co-organizer of open mic evenings.

Supriya Omi

Supriya is a Science graduate but loves arts equally. Writing has always been more of her passion than just a hobby. She says creativity keeps her sane and she relates scientific facts with arts to create her pieces of art.

She is a strong believer of the fact that writing is a powerful tool by which one can bring a change in the mindset of people. Words have power to heal and make a difference.

Riya

Riya is a business student who likes to explore and experiment with painting, poetry and many more adventures.

She's an individual with insatiable curiosity and would love to answer your questions and discuss stuff like menstruation, economics, art or random objects like fans and ice.

Dr. Smita Todkar

Smita has three years of experience in public health sector. She holds Bachelor of Ayurvedic Medicine and Surgery (B.A.M.S.) degree followed by Master in Public health (MPH).

She works with 'Ekjut India' a non-profit organization in Jharkhand, India. She's also a principle investigator for ongoing project named, 'Participatory Learning and Action focusing on Menstrual Hygiene among the adolescent girls within urban poor areas of Ranchi, Jharkhand, India'.

Dr Smita also has a working experience as Medical Officer (M.O.) with different organizations in rural and tribal areas of Maharashtra, Odisha and Bihar.

Swati Kansra

Swati Kansra has been the university topper in both her Bachelors' and Masters' degree in Multimedia from BBK DAV College for Women, Amritsar. She has a teaching experience of 6 years while being an active participant in several seminar and conferences.

She is the author of the book "Fundamentals of Multimedia" and also has many research papers based on technology and visual media to her credit.

She loves to keep herself updated on knowledge of all new technology.

Akhila Rajesh

Akhila Rajesh is an IT professional with poetry at her heart. Her journey with poetry began in her school days and continues to get intriguing each passing day.

Her first published book of poems is – 'From Womb to World'. The second book 'Enchanted Verses' was a collaboration with fellow colleagues. Her poems have also been published in multiple anthologies of Poetry Society of India, Xpress Publications, The Significant League, Poetry Corner, Asian Literary Society etc.

KNOW THE EDITOR

Samridhi Aneja

Samridhi Aneja has been working as a freelance graphic designer from 4 years and has designed for publishing houses, startups, NGOs, schools, solo-preneurs and event managers in India. Currently guiding design interns for Kadam, she is also a published co-author of many books based on poetry, research and dialogue and has delivered online and offline workshops and lectures on 'creative writing and aesthetics in design' for schools and organizations alike during the past couple of years.

She is a proud period positivism advocate who is currently conducting the "PCOS Emotional Responses' Survey." She had also been instrumental in managing and executing with Kadam, an online nation-wide campaign and competition called 'The Period Art Wave' which was based upon period visual art.

She believes in the power of politeness and the three magical words 'thank you, sorry and please' in every aspect and phase of life. She finds bliss and sense of freedom in writing and loves observing visual art of all sorts.

KNOW THE ILLUSTRATOR

Shishir Kant Bhuyan

Shishir Kant Bhuyan, who comes from a Jamshedpur is a data science professional and a freelance illustration artist working in various media. His paintings have been featured in various platforms and websites. He is also an avid urban sketcher. Over the years his paintings have been exhibited in galleries like Rangoli metro art center and Tagore society of arts.

Most of his paintings are an expression of his imagination and feelings. He likes to tell stories about hope and the beauty in nature through his paintings. You can look more of his work on his Instagram : @shishirkart and email him at shishirkart@gmail.com